RED ORBIT

A CHRISTIAN SCIENCE FICTION BY

ETHAN RUEDLINGER

Author:
Author Ethan Ruedlinger

Editors:
Paula Savanah Ruedlinger
Connie Lynn Ruedlinger
Leonard Wayne Ruedlinger

This book is dedicated to all those who ponder the inner workings of the cosmos in hopes that God will reveal His creation to them. Remain in Christ, and one day you will gain what you've sought.

TABLE OF CONTENTS

Chapter 1: The Station. 1

Chapter 2: MOSS Cavern. 30

Chapter 3: The Bermuda Tunnel. . . . 44

Chapter 4: Into The Maw. 59

Chapter 5: An Alien World. 67

Chapter 6: City Of Devils. 73

Chapter 7: The Hat Man. 88

Chapter 8: Unmasked. 101

Chapter 9: Refuting Deception. . . . 114

Chapter 10: The Return 139

Chapter 11: Preparations. 157

Chapter 12: MOSS Colony. 171

Chapter 13: Scouting Mission. 182

Chapter 14: The Assistant Director. . . 196

Chapter 15: Interstellar Advancements. . 214

PREFACE

This US Government document is being declassified for interstellar publication as a work of historical significance. The following document is a transcription of the long-classified official logbook of Dr. John Duncan of the original 2097 Mars Orbital Space Station crew. Dr. Duncan, the great grandson of Edward G. Duncan of the 2nd American Revolution, was a leading figure in the early Martian colonization effort, and worked to establish the very first human colonial settlement on the planet, elevating mankind to an interplanetary species. Dr. Duncan also made several important scientific discoveries in the process, furthering the durability and technological capability of United States spacecraft. America wishes to preserve his legacy as an early interstellar pioneer for the educational benefit of future generations. To maintain US interstellar security, certain aspects of this work will remain classified indefinitely, and will therefore be redacted. -Silas Duncan, USDIH Director, 05/28/2278

This Book Is An Official Publication Of The United States Department Of Intergalactic History, Formerly Organized As A Subsidiary Of The United States Department Of Interstellar Colonization.

MMCXVII DIH-953 U/FOUO 22780528

CHAPTER 1

THE STATION

"The future of humanity is going to bifurcate in two directions: Either it's going to become multiplanetary, or it's going to remain confined to one planet and eventually there's going to be an extinction event." -Elon Musk

Entry 1: 3/31/2099
To clarify the situation surrounding the future entries of my log, allow me to recall a bit of history, and record for you what has occurred thus far, as well as give a bit of background information regarding my involvement in this interplanetary endeavor.

Since the very creation of the world, mankind has gazed upon the stars in awe and wonder, with a longing to one day understand them. When mankind first landed on

the moon nearly 130 years ago, a
fire ignited in the hearts of
millions of Americans, a longing
to further explore the cosmos and
conquer them just as their
ancestors had conquered the
various territories and lands of
Earth. Their generation, and a few
subsequent however, were the
middle children of history. From
around 1940-2078, humanity endured
a period of limbo, for lack of a
better term. These men were born
far too late to explore even the
final frontiers remaining on
Earth, yet were born much too
early to explore the stars. For
many decades, America, as well as
the rest of the western world, had
been ruled by inferior men who
sought wealth and authority over
the wellbeing of the citizens they
were charged with serving. There
was a massive and worldwide effort
on the part of many global
organizations

    working together to
systematically enslave the free
world as a whole through
diplomatic policies disguised as
being beneficial, yet were nothing
more than means to an end. Both
sides of every free nation's
political aisle were nothing more
than controlled opposition, and
behind America's back, they would
scheme against the world as one
united global party, a globalist
cabal. Despite their many tactics,
the American populace eventually
caught on. American society was on
the brink of collapse in the
2030's, and by 2038, the Second
Revolutionary War had begun. This
same war spread to Canada,
England, Ireland, Scotland, Wales,
Germany, France; millions of
citizens of every western nation,
like my great grandfather Edward
G. Duncan, put aside their
differences and banded together as
a unitary fighting force to
dismantle their authoritarian
regime for the 3

future of their descendants.
After a few years of the single
bloodiest war in human history,
America once again entered a
prosperous and morally upright era
of enlightenment as the world's
uncontested superpower, and with
the archeological discoveries made
during the war solidifying the
historicity and accuracy of the
Biblical narrative, the world
followed. As the decades rolled,
technology advanced, and
interplanetary travel was
eventually feasible, and later
realized. In 2078, NASA was able
to send a manned orbiter to Mars.
While these men couldn't land on
the surface of the planet, this
still represented a historically
unprecedented leap for mankind. In
2084, NASA launched a new program
with the sole intention of
terraforming and colonizing Mars.
Researching the planet from orbit
was their first step. They spent

nearly a decade building an orbital space station and equipping it with drop pods, artificial gravity-generation technology, every bell and whistle they could to ensure researchers studying the planet from orbit would have some level of comfortability.

The year was 2097 Anno Domini. Humanity had begun colonizing Mars and had set up greenhouses for terraformation. The MOSS consists of three large wings that rotate in such a way as to generate artificial gravity. The MOSS (Mars Orbital Space Station) is home to many world renowned scientists and astrophysicists who have embarked on a quest to study Mars' planetary conditions in hopes of optimizing future colonists' terraformation efforts. The men on board are of varying backgrounds and skillsets, but each of them have left their lives back on earth to support humanity's quest to spread life across the galaxy one planet at a time. These scientists are hard at work studying potential solutions a variety of hurdles they must overcome in colonization. The red planet's lack of a magnetic field to deflect harmful solar radiation emitted from the sun is one of their primary concerns. As a graduate of many prestigious universities and a Doctor of Astrophysics, as well as a 20-year employee of NASA, it was only natural that I would be offered the chance to contribute my expertise to this endeavor. As an unmarried man with no children to speak of, it wasn't a difficult decision for me to accept NASA's offer to become a Martian orbital researcher.

I'll begin my retelling of recent events with Dr. Brogg.

As Brogg was pouring over the notes my research team left on his desk, he came to a sudden realization…

"You've calculated this wrong!" Brogg said, angrily ripping up the spreadsheet that I, John Duncan, the head of the research team, had worked tirelessly to curate. Our current goal, as previously eluded to, was to create an artificial magnetic field capable of deflecting the sun's harmful radiation, and Dr. Brogg had placed me at the forefront of the operation. Dr. Brogg was a short, hefty man who was never seen without a grey suit and tie. He was a connoisseur of fine Cuban cigars, and would often indulge in them while working in his office. I've typically been described by my peers as a tall, lanky man who usually wears simple jeans and a collared shirt. Unbeknownst to me, Brogg had discovered that my data

I'd gathered from my laboratory-simulated magnetic field was incorrectly recorded, and was rendered useless for any further decomposition.

"We have until December of 2098 to complete this project, Mr. Duncan. How do you suppose your department will reach any of it's goals if you continue to fumble these spreadsheets? Record your results correctly!" I apologized to my boss and acknowledged my error before heading back to the lab for another round of crucial test runs.

From data I'd gathered during my time studying the earth's magnetic field through seismic and magnetic measurement instruments inserted close to the core of our home planet, Earth, I had compiled a blueprint of a machine capable of artificially generating a magnetic field. Prior to leading my team to intricately design and assemble each component of this massive engineering feat, I began studying the effects of a prototype small-scale artificial magnetic field in hopes of replicating the design on a larger scale. As I studied each set of data I'd recorded, I slowly began blueprinting the device needed to begin terraforming Mars. The project was an eventual success, as I gathered enough data to produce a prototype full-scale artificial magnetic field generator by the end of 2098, as projected.

"Congratulations, John! Accurate, and on time!" Dr. Brogg began. "It isn't easy coordinating with a team that isn't familiar with your leadership style, but I believe you're the most qualified leader aboard the MOSS. That's why I've chosen you for a newly-created leadership role. From this day forward, you'll be referred to by your subordinates as Commander

Duncan. You will coordinate and lead hands-on planetside operations. I will, however, still have final authority, of course." My growing excitement flooded into my expression as my eyes widened, and I struggled to contain my grin. "Thank you so much, Dr. Brogg! I'll do everything in my power to continue advancing our colonization efforts!" "That's what I like to hear!" Dr. Brogg exclaimed, seemingly displaying a genuine smile for once. His strange new demeanor was off-putting to me, as I had long since taken Dr. Brogg as nothing more than an eccentric brainiac. Brogg isn't the kind of man you'd expect to be so kind and cordial considering his inherent antisocial nature, but perhaps he was warming up to me.

The next project that Dr. Brogg left on my desk was to set up and run the newly-engineered solar-powered Martian magnetic field generation system, as well as discovering what potentially useful metals and materials were commonly occurring within the network of cave systems known to exist under the crust of Mars. As astroid mining isn't even technologically or economically feasible yet, gathering resources from Martian cave systems may prove to be pivotal in our colonization campaign.

I prepared my team of researchers to enter the Martian atmosphere via a manned self-propelled atmospheric probe. The probe was capable of moving freely about the atmosphere using cutting-edge gravity-resistant technology. Rather than relying solely on traditional propulsion methods to maintain orbit in atmosphere, the probe utilized the aforementioned quantum gravity-resistant technology that would nearly eliminate the effect that gravity would normally have on the probe, thus allowing it to move freely about the Martian skies. I had decided that I'd select my most resilient and intelligent men for this particular mission, men with varying skill sets, experiences, and backgrounds. Those I'd determined to be best suited for the endeavor were Michael, Henry, Jeremy, and Nehemiah.

Michael and Jeremy are both tall and lanky, with similar builds to myself. Michael is very quiet and reserved, a morally upstanding man in his early 20's who knows humility, while Jeremy, who is in his mid 20's, has a more aggressive and pompous demeanor, which I dreaded putting up with. If it weren't for Jeremy's extensive knowledge of chemical sciences, I wouldn't have even considered allowing him to tag

along. Michael has an incredible
knack for geology and seismology,
which would prove invaluable.
Henry is an older, wiser man with
ever-greying hair and an often
stoic expression, however, even
the wisdom that typically displays
upon his face couldn't hide the
years of anguish that had torn him
down piece by piece. The two wars
he'd endured back on earth are
visible in every wrinkle on his
aging face.

Nehemiah is a man after God's
own heart, a young Christian
Evangelist who strives to love
both God and man. He is in his
30's, about 6'1 and of an average
weight. He would give thanks to
God for every little good thing
that occurred in his life, and
would praise God through the worst
of life's storms. He possesses an
extensive understanding of
biology, astronomy, and
astrophysics.

Science had all but proven the validity of the gospel accounts and the sheer importance of faith in the Lord, and billions of earth's inhabitants have been devout Christians for decades.

The crew loaded their bags onto the probe and buckled into their seats located in the cockpit. I had brought along an experimental gravity-altering device that would allow us to traverse through steep cave systems with ease. The device was designed to act as a handheld iteration of the intricate gravity-resistance system present within the engine of the probe. I had also brought along every sort of traditional caving gear I could find on the MOSS. This mission was a significant undertaking, and success was pertinent, so I ensured my crew and I were ready for anything.

As the probe detached from the MOSS's pod storage system, my crew and I began our decent into the lower layers of the Martian atmosphere. I activated the gravity-resistance system to maintain orbit merely a few thousand feet above the surface of the planet. For nearly a decade, we'd been aware of a particular entrance to a sizable cave system which could potentially harbor the much-needed metals and materials that my team was searching for. We waited until our probe was directly above the approximate location of the entrance before I shut the gravity-resistance system down, and began descending to the surface.

"LZ in sight, extending landing gear now!" Henry's voice boomed.

"We're about to smack the ground and die if John's the one operating this thing." Jeremy said defiantly.

"I've been courteous to you so far, Jeremy, don't push your

luck." I warned sternly.

I had previously dealt with cases of insubordination, and was well acquainted with Jeremy's track record of ignoring orders and endangering the lives of the crews he'd served with on previous missions. I knew the only way to keep Jeremy in line was to chastise him for his antics to shut them down as soon as they arose.

As Henry extended the landing gear, I monitored the various instruments on the control panel as we touched down on the surface of the red planet. After Jeremy ensured it was safe to exit the craft, we extended the ramp and jumped one by one into the dirt, climbing gear in hand. We promptly assembled the artificial magnetic field generator, and ensured it was fully functional before moving on to the second half of our mission.

As we approached the crater, I began to feel an overwhelming sense of unease, as if there were some sort of unseen being that was present, warning me to turn back while I still had my life. Electing not to indulge this seemingly random sense of dread, I led my team into the maw of the great Martian cave. "Considering this cave system hasn't been given a proper name, and we're the first to explore it, perhaps we should be given the honor of naming it." Michael said excitedly, as we made our descent into the first section of the cave.

"Perhaps we could name it the 'MOSS System.'" Nehemiah suggested.

"That seems a bit unimaginative, does it not?" Jeremy said mockingly.

"Why not name it 'The Maw Of Death?'" Henry inquired.

"I'd rather not proclaim such

doom." I expressed, already exasperated from Jeremy's incessant stupidity. "'MOSS Cavern' is an appropriate name for this cave system, let's go with that." This was the most we'd spoken since we left the station, and it seemed things may remain that way for the duration of the mission, considering Jeremy had raised tensions.

As we ventured further into the cave, we discovered that the system was considerably larger than previous studies had shown. We examined several pits littered throughout the innards of the cave, some were seemingly bottomless pits that were of no use to us. There were a few minor ice deposits around the edges of many of the pits, which we drew samples of for later research. We ventured further still, and discovered that the cavernous expanse that lay before us

18

appeared rich in various minerals exposed at the surface of the rock. We found stalactites protruding from the ceiling of the cavern in all directions, made of a strange, (what we assumed to be) naturally formed alloy similar in appearance to stainless steel. They didn't appear as any stalactites common to earth's cave systems, rather, they were much more round and bulbous in appearance. The few crystalline-structured stalagmites also present before us glistened in the dim glow of our lanterns. It was quite a marvelous and unexpected sight to behold. Nehemiah scratched his chin, his mouth agape in disbelief as Michael and I swiftly equipped our testing kits and began working to discover what sort of minerals occurred nearby. The potential that the metal alloy we'd discovered, and even the astronomically large cave system itself wasn't formed by natural means had occurred to me in the inner recesses of my thoughts, however, I suppressed the notion out of sheer disbelief, and perhaps also due to the potential implications of such a discovery should it become known.

After running rigorous automated tests on various mineral samples using an advanced electronic machine commonly referred to as a "geolometer", a handy, all-encompassing, automated geologic analysis tool, my fear, and perhaps even my desire to a certain extent, was realized; These "minerals" were metal alloys more complex than we'd initially assumed, so much so that the possibility of them occurring naturally was unthinkable. They were composed of a mixture of nickel, iron, ███████, and four other metals not known to exist within the realm of science.

Nearly questioning the accuracy of my geolometer, I concluded that we'd not only just discovered four new metals, but a strange and powerful alloy that could, for all we knew, have been impervious to anything.

"John!" Henry's voice boomed across the cold, reflective metal of the cave. "I'm beginning to suspect that not only was this cave system created by some form of intelligent life, but it may not be a cave system at all, but an ancient structure of some sort." "If that's the case…" I questioned intently, "then how would you reconcile the obvious stalactite formations with your theory?" "According to simulations performed on my geolometer, due to the alloy's molecular structure, if this particular material were to reach it's melting point, while drooping from a ceiling, it would create these bulbous formations that are present above our very heads!" Henry exclaimed. "It would've also congealed into a crystalline structure if melted closer to the ground as seen in these stalagmites." "This is melted steel?" I inquired, still not convinced. "Sort of. It's not steel per se, but a complex alloy that cannot by damaged by any conventional means besides exposure to an inconceivable level of heat upwards of 80,000°F. If we deconstruct the nature of this alloy and replicate it on a large scale, we could produce a shuttle capable of passing through the surface of the sun. Think of the impact this could have on heliophysics!" For some reason that I can't quite mentally deconstruct, I overlooked the implications of the fact that this alloy which had a melting point of 80,000°F was clearly *melted* within a freezing Martian cave!

Considering the technological leaps and bounds our discovery was certain to achieve, we all began cheering joyously, eager to report our findings to our colleagues on the MOSS. "God has gifted us with an incredible blessing today!" Nehemiah shouted, his voice booming throughout the cavern. "Imagine the applications, the technological leaps and bounds that are sure to arise from this discovery!" Nehemiah continued.

"Let's extract a few larger samples and return to the station. It's best if we return later, less ill-equipped to safely traverse… whatever we've stumbled upon." I ordered.

"Let's not be so hasty." Jeremy said defiantly. "I'm going to explore the cave a bit more. Let's see what else we can uncover, John. You order us to leave immediately as though you're terrified of what might lie beyond

23

where we stand. Don't be such a cowardly waste of intellect. After such an astounding success, we can certainly afford to throw a little risk into the mission for the sake of progress."

Having quite enough of Jeremy's insubordination and realizing how dangerous and irresponsible such an idea could prove to be given our lack of proper equipment, I *hastily* ordered Jeremy, as well as the rest of the men to collect what samples they were able, and return to the MOSS. Using an older model solar laser (of which I can't recall the manufacturer's name) developed sometime in the 2050's, we carefully cut sections of the alloy to bring to our research station. However seemingly irrational it may have been, I felt that somewhere in that cave, there lay the presence of some unperceived danger.

Log Entry 2: 5/9/2099

Nearly a month rolled by without incident. I haven't written anything in this log since that day, I've been busy with studying our groundbreaking discovery. After subjecting the alloy samples to various well-advanced technological studies, we concluded that it would be possible, albeit difficult, to replicate the exact conditions in which this alloy would form on a large enough scale to produce an "invincible" coating for interstellar vehicles, if only there were any known natural occurrences of the four newly-discovered metals to conduct further research upon. We simply could not deduce the molecular structure, nor the exact conditions in which to replicate the creation of the metals, only that it was theoretically possible to replicate. This barred us from

creating the alloy by artificial
means, and the only known possible
means of obtaining it, to my utter
dismay, lies within MOSS Cavern.
After several meetings on the
subject with Dr. Brogg, we reached
the conclusion that the best
course of action would be to
classify all information
pertaining to the very existence
of this alloy and the four metals
as Top Secret, and to keep the
operation under wraps. Dr. Brogg
was also deeply favoring the idea
of exploring the cave for the
potential natural occurrence of
the 4 metals, something I was
dreading, yet knew was inevitable.
We now knew that the samples we'd
recovered belonged to some form of
artificially created structure,
perhaps the ruins of some ancient
"invincible" ship. However, with
no possible understanding of who
or what could've created the
structure, we refrained from

jumping to conclusions, and simply took our findings as is. Realizing that any automated mining mission would need to be manned in order to ensure the cavern is further explored without incident, Brogg commissioned a myriad of mining gear, along with a fleet of mining rovers to accompany us on our return trip to MOSS Cavern, as it was now officially named, thanks to my input. Due to the many unknowns regarding the origin of the newly discovered, potentially alien structure, Brogg also commissioned hypersonic M1A96 rifles newly developed by the US Government in 2096. These rifles were the official successor to the original hypersonic R89H40 rifles developed in 2040 that were equipped with nano-nuclear munitions capable of traveling at 20x the speed of sound. As these were immediately mass manufactured for the US

Military, the concept was repeatedly improved and expanded upon throughout the later decades in an effort to keep the American military technologically advanced, leading to the creation of the R57B2 Handgun System in 2056 for use by military officers, as well as the M4A1776. Proudly released for the US Tricentennial in 2076, this rifle was capable of eliminating a target from nearly any distance with minimal noise, minimal recoil, and astronomical accuracy. It was also the current service rifle in the arms rooms of most military companies and batteries, as the laughably outdated R89H40 was nearly phased out. Perhaps the most interesting weapon system that has recently been developed is the ███████, a classified ████ ██████████ when the ██████ ███████.

Long gone are the days when the US Government would seek after the lowest bidder when choosing a weapons manufacturer, it was mandated in 2043 that the government was required to accept only the most high-quality of weaponry that would result from the highest-quality contract, to ensure the safety and longevity of those actively serving in ongoing wars in the armed forces.

The brand new standard-issue M1A98 Rifle utilizes the newly advanced "RCSS" (recoil compensation and silencing system), which gives this weapon less recoil than a BB gun, while rendering each round fired dead silent. I was satisfied with the equipment requisitions Dr. Brogg had made, and felt safer knowing that I would at least be accompanied by 4 other armed men that I felt I could ultimately trust with my life.

CHAPTER 2

MOSS CAVERN

"The very cave you fear to enter holds the treasure that you seek." -Joseph Campbell

Entry 3: 5/10/2099

I promptly assembled my team, selecting Henry, Jeremy, Nehemiah, and Michael once more for the journey, considering they knew what to expect. We gathered our gear, tucked it carefully into the various storage compartments of our rover, and entered the drop pod to descend into the Martian atmosphere and make our landing next to MOSS Cavern.

Once we'd arrived on site, we activated the fleet of mining rovers and sent them into the maw of MOSS Cavern ahead of ourselves, with a live video feed from the leading scouting rover viewable on

a handheld device. Entering the
cave, we immediately noticed that
our bootprints we'd left in the
dirt on our previous mission were
disturbed. They appeared to be
brushed over, with no apparent
traces of the culprit. None of our
mining rovers had rolled through
the area, and as far as we knew,
we were the only human beings
present on Mars. Puzzled, I told
Michael and Jeremy to investigate
a diverging tunnel near the maw in
which we sent four mining rovers
while Henry, Nehemiah, and I would
continue along the main system.
Once we'd reached the newly
discovered alloy, we elected to
continue following our huge fleet
of rovers deeper into the
unexplored cavern rather than hang
back and view the exploration
remotely. As we ventured deeper,
the alloy cut off beyond a certain
distance, suddenly transitioning
back to a mundane, dust-filled

cave. After venturing deeper
still, we'd approached a wall, in
which there was a small gap just
large enough for the rovers to
roll through, and just large
enough for us to scrunch down and
squeeze through ourselves. Once
we'd entered through the opening,
we found ourselves face to face
with a large, fish bowl shaped
cave, with a few small holes in
the ceiling through which sunlight
beamed across the otherwise dimly
illuminated "room." Confused as to
why this was the apparent end of
the cavern since our geolometer
readings predicted the cave to be
dozens of times larger, we began
running tests and searching the
room. We discovered that the cave
wall to the right was hollow, as
if something, or someone had
intentionally built it to hide or
cover something. We decided to use
an M1A98 round to blow through it.
We pulled our rovers out of the

room and squeezed back through the hole. Promptly exiting after examining the area, I pushed my rifle through the opening and fired one round at the hollow wall. After the round detonated upon impact, the entire room immediately went up in smoke and dust. To ensure our safety, we waited a solid 10 minutes for it to settle.

We then entered the room, discovering that the cave wall had been hiding a much more massive room. When I entered and gazed at the sheer size of it, I questioned wether it was the size of the planet itself. The cave room was dimly lit by the faint glow of our devices. The air was dense, and had a sort of moist texture about it.

As we explored, we began to realize that the massive cavernous expanse we'd found ourselves in was, simply, a cave. There wasn't anything intrinsically different or interesting about the large "room" other than its size. We sent a scouting drone out to scan and digitally map the area, and throughout the entire length of the cave, the only anomaly seemed to be two tunnels. One led deeper into the Martian crust, theoretically cutting into the mantle in a rather mundane, natural formation that, for all we knew, could've spanned the planet. The other, however, led to something that the drone was unable to map. It was as if the drone had malfunctioned upon entering it. We decided to send in two of our rovers to investigate, but the feed on our devices disconnected not long after they'd entered, which indicated that the rovers had either shut down or malfunctioned without any prior indication of an issue, which is highly unusual given the sophisticated diagnostics system each one was equipped with. We decided to leave the two rovers behind and return to the MOSS to report to Dr. Brogg and seek his advice on how to pursue exploration of this potentially dangerous area, but not before collecting several more chunks of the myserteous alloy on our way out, enough to utilize for building a sophisticated "invincible" spacecraft.

Once we exited the cavern, we gathered our supplies, pulled our rovers into our pod, and took an uneventful ride back to the MOSS. Dr. Brogg was eagerly awaiting us back on the ship, fascinated and bewildered by our discovery of the potentially hazardous cave opening. He was by no means angry that we'd left one of our rovers planetside, and even commended me for taking the initiative to ensure the safety of my team.

After convening with Brogg and other prominent scientists belonging to various fields of study, they decided to message NASA's headquarters back on Earth to not only report our findings, but to seek further guidance from mission control. We aren't subject to their authority, but we all acknowledge that this is uncharted territory that no man has ever ventured through, it's certainly best to involve them. My personal guess is that they'll utilize some form of radiation-proof remote exploratory craft controlled from earth to explore the newly discovered cave, but who knows?

Entry 4: 6/8/2099

It's been a few weeks since I last logged anything. Earth's mainstream media has been abuzz with a new "miracle cure" drug that supposedly not only cures the majority of neurological ailments,

but enhances the brain's cognitive abilities beyond the normal human capacity. The manufacturer claimed that those of a "mentally challenged" IQ were able to gain the intelligence of a college graduate with a single treatment. It seems technological advancement is rapidly accelerating, which will hopefully continue to benefit us in ways currently unforeseen. We also sent what samples we had acquired back to Earth aboard a pod, and they've already not only replicated the process by which the presumably unnaturally formed alloy was created, but they've built an unmanned craft heavily coated with

the alloy which could
theoretically explore not only the
violent environments of gas giants
in our solar system, but the sun
itself. They're planning a solar
exploration mission in two weeks,
I'm rather excited myself to
witness this event unfold.

Entry 5: 6/9/2099

We've mostly been resting up from the mission. I believe Dr. Brogg has something planned for us, but I'm not exactly sure what. Perhaps another manned mission. Brogg mentioned establishing a base of operations on the surface right next to the cavern to study the strange "alien craft." All information pertaining to our discovery is still classified as of now, even the alloy coating of the solar craft remains undisclosed, but I'm inclined to think that they'll want to release this to the public as soon as we know more.

Entry 6: 6/17/2099

Its been a few days since I've written. I've been praying for a sign as to what we should tackle next. I was told by Dr. Brogg that I'm set to receive a few awards, including a Nobel Prize for my discovery, but I told him I'd refuse unless the rest of my team would be awarded the same, to which he replied: "That can certainly be arranged, John." I sincerely hope so, they were just as much a part of our ground-breaking discovery and deserve international (or perhaps *interplanetary…*) recognition for their work.

Dr. Brogg is diverting his attention from the cave for the time being in anticipation of a response from NASA and other earth-side authorities. We're instead focusing on implementing another terraformation strategy involving the use of over 500 advanced warehouse-sized CO2 converters that would, in theory and according to multiple simulations conducted on our systems, convert 22% of the Martian atmosphere into oxygen in less that 6 months. We will also be using 250 Artificial Atom-Targeted Nuclear Co2-N2 Transmuters to convert 71% of the martian atmosphere to Nitrogen, since the Martian atmosphere is already currently comprised of 3% nitrogen, and Earth's atmosphere is comprised of approximately 78% Nitrogen, and 21% Oxygen. We aim to allow a 1% differential of oxygen levels to ensure atmospheric stability and the health of human, animal, and plant life. Our newly developed nuclear transmuters are capable of converting copious amounts of different gas's atomic nuclei through protonic bombardment, to alter their atomic structure

through a precise and targeted
process, thereby converting them
into any needed gaseous material
such as oxygen or nitrogen gas.

Entry 7: 7/4/2099

We've spent an exorbitant amount of time setting up these machines on the surface through a series of manned missions, and they're now fully functional thanks not only to the well-rounded expertise of Dr. Brogg and Jeremy, but of the several crews of incredibly gifted engineers and craftsmen who assisted us in this exciting endeavor. I owe them my sincerest gratitude, as I am just as excited as anyone for the terraformation and colonization of Mars, especially considering my ongoing involvement in this venture. Today, we're not only celebrating the birth of our nation, but the success we've experienced so far.

CHAPTER 3

THE BERMUDA TUNNEL

"A bit of science distances one from God, but much science nears one to Him. Posterity will one day laugh at the foolishness of modern materialistic philosophers. The more I study nature, the more I stand amazed at the work of our Creator. I pray while I am engaged at my work in the laboratory." -Louis Pasteur

Entry 8: 10/2/2099
It's been a couple months, the martian atmospheric oxygen and nitrogen levels have been rising at a rate previously thought to be impossible by any artificial means. I've decided to log this new entry because Dr. Brogg has received word from NASA that they are planning another manned exploratory mission into the strange opening within MOSS Cavern. They've formally requested

that we begin preparations for
exploring and further mapping the
cave system so we can utilize
whatever resources are discovered
within. I've unofficially decided
that I'll once again be selecting
each of the members of the
previous team, Henry, Jeremy,
Nehemiah, and Michael; to take
this journey with me. Brogg also
casually mentioned setting up an
automated mining station within
the area of the cavern containing
the new alloy. Considering this
method to potentially be more
efficient than replicating the
alloy on Earth, NASA is planning
to use it to build the first-ever
manned solar exploratory craft, as
well as potentially using the
material in the future to build a
craft capable of faster-than-light
travel once the technology comes
to fruition.

Entry 9: 10/4/2099

I've spoken with my crew regarding our return trip. They've been briefed on our objective. Our mode of transportation and means of exploration will remain the same, our rover fleet will be significantly smaller, however. As previously stated, our main objective is to set up an automated mining rig within the cave to harvest the heat-resistant metal we've discovered. Our unofficial objective is to explore the cavernous offshoot from the large fish bowl shaped cave. On our previous visit, we blew down a wall-like formation to access the larger cave, and discovered those two strange wormhole-like caverns carved into the wall of the seemingly infinite void of a cave. Our instruments determined that one of them bored deep into the Martian mantle, well below the crust. I intend to fully explore the other, which appears to be impossible to map with the various methods we attempted to utilize. The dark "hole" which seems impossible to illuminate also seems to distort, and eventually jam all comms systems and disable any electronic equipment that enters. The idea of the new alloy being the remnants of some form of ancient Martian craft has been swirling around in my head. I've remained relatively professional in these writings, but I feel this pertains to the overall terraformation and colonization experiment and is therefore worthy of being recorded. I've been stricken with severe bouts of insomnia over the previous few nights. The lifeless cavern, devoid of all light and sound, with an air of the remnants or essence of some otherworldly entity, somehow assaults my senses with any attempt at rest. I've

considered consulting Dr. Brogg
for a psych eval, however, last
night, my senses were once again
assaulted, yet with a strange
vision unlike any of the previous.
Before me flashed variations of
unfathomable entities, with forms
so incomprehensible that it was
impossible for my eyes to focus on
them. Strange, unintelligible
figures danced about in a
ritualistic fashion akin to a kind
of occult activity. It was so
profoundly ethereal that it
couldn't possibly have been a
meticulous fabrication of the
mind. I'm convinced that some sort
of object existing within our
material realm is somehow
interacting with or manipulating
my cognition to such a degree as
to produce these idiosyncratic
conceptualizations which haven't
ceased to interrupt my leisure
time. As you can surely deduce,
that object would have to lie

within MOSS Cavern. If my hypothesis is merely hogwash, I will gladly bear the full weight of my decision to remain silent on this issue. I like to consider myself a man of rationality and common sense, but I have an unyielding, seemingly primal intuition regarding this idea. It simply feels as though it couldn't possibly be untrue in any sense. I'll update this log with a new entry once we return from our mission.

Entry 10: 11/08/2100

I've returned, though blindsided
by an enigmatic series of events
that have surely altered the
course of human history. I remain
unconvinced that any retelling of
the events of the previous month
could capture the sheer insanity
of what has transpired. I truly
hope this log is not classified
upon entry into US Government
records, though I'm certain it is
now inevitable. I'm still reeling
from everything, let me compose
myself and start from the
beginning.

It was an unusually serene day
here aboard the MOSS, I was giving
myself a refresher course on some
of the fundamental aspects of
geology when Dr. Brogg entered my
office, informing me that it was
now time to gather the
aforementioned crew that has
accompanied me on each of these
missions, and move all of our

equipment to the drop pod on the opposite end of the station. This was becoming routing for my crew and I, we simply executed each step in our mission as we had each previous time.

We made our descent through the Martian atmosphere, landing directly in front of the entrance to MOSS Cavern. We pulled our rovers off the pod and saddled them up with our spelunking gear before entering the cave once again. Henry insisted that he take the lead considering this could potentially be a dangerous and arduous journey once we'd entered the tubular cave. Two days prior, when discussing it with Henry and Michael, we'd agreed to refer to it as "The Bermuda Tunnel" due to it's strange properties seemingly congruent with the "Bermuda Triangle."

We directed the rovers to set up the mining rig within minutes.

While they worked at the start
of the cave among the glistening
crystalline stalactite and
stalagmite formations, we ventured
further still in an attempt to
accomplish our secondary
objective, accompanied by only a
single rover.

Upon making his way into the
large, fish-bowl like cave, Henry
stopped dead in his tracks and
glanced back at me. "Every nerve
in my body is screaming at me to
turn back." he said in a nervous
tone. "Perhaps it would be best if
we informed Dr. Brogg that we were
unable to complete our objectives
as required. There's nothing here
worth dying for." "We have no
choice but to explore The Bermuda
Tunnel on foot, our electronics
are fried the second they make
contact with whatever form of
radiation is present within." I
told him, almost convincing myself
that we should press onward. As

I've made abundantly clear, I was all too familiar with the strange, instinctual, gut-wrenching feeling he was referring to. It felt as though we were preparing to charge an enemy garrison head-on through automatic gunfire, and it was accompanied by battle jitters. I could clearly tell Jeremy, Nehemiah, and Michael were all feeling the same. Not long after we all managed to squeeze into the fishbowl cave, we heard a loud, rumbling echo throughout the dark bowl, permeating through the ground below us, and vibrating our boots in a punctuated manner. The walls of the cave began rattling violently, and the entrance to the fishbowl cave collapsed, sealing our only exit in mounds of rubble. Dumbfounded, we sent out two scouting drones equipped with sophisticated instruments similar to those within our geolometers.

We were hoping to detect some sort of seismic or volcanic activity, something we could pin the blame on for this sudden onset of strange movement. As expected, when the drones returned, they reported that no such activity was detected, and no alternate routes existed anywhere within the fishbowl aside from the two tunnels. I made the all-too-hasty determination that it was worth the risk to attempt to blast through the rock with our M1A98 rifles. After attempting to fire four different cartridges, clearing the mag well and bolt carrier of any debris, checking the firing pin, and using three different magazines, I realized that not a single one of our rounds would fire, which was concerning, to say the least. I simply chocked it up to defective ammunition, and logged an incident report for Dr. Brogg. We still had contact with the rovers that were actively establishing the automated mining rig, so we knew it was very likely that they could be redirected to relocate the debris and clear the exit at any time, giving us peace of mind for the time being.

Venturing further still, we approached the tunnel in it's pitch-black, treacherous mystique. After a lengthy discussion involving drones and explosives, we finally agreed to send our single remaining rover equipped with a Geiger Counter into The Bermuda Tunnel as it broadcast a live video feed to our devices, as a form a preliminary exploration, mainly to ensure that we could safely enter the tunnel without being instantaneously fried by radiation.

The rover's Geiger Counter was unable to detect a hint of radiation up until the feed was

cut off. Strangely, the rover
managed to push further than the
previous few we'd sent on the
autonomous exploratory mission.
The only thing that was evident
from analyzing the feed is that,
though we remotely flashed several
of the various lights installed on
the rover into the tunnel,
including lasers and infrared,
there was not a single visible
beam of light anywhere but on the
rover itself. Even the walls had
effectively rendered themselves
invisible by somehow absorbing
every last photon of light they
came into contact with, despite
being detected and mapped by
geologic instruments which mainly
function via the distinct
fluctuation of high-pitched sound
waves. Highly intrigued by this,
once the rover had ceased to
respond, we gathered our gear and
prepared to enter. Upon turning to
choose which of my men would enter

56

first, with the idea that I
would volunteer planted firmly in
the back of my mind, I noticed
that Michael was not present.
Considering he was our junior
member, I immediately waxed
concerned. Aghast, I gave the area
an inquisitive sweep with my eyes,
attempting to ascertain his
position within the cave, quickly
realizing the sheer futility of a
cave-wide search in an area the
size of a mountain range. Henry,
Jeremy, Nehemiah and I began
clamoring to find him, shrieking
and bellowing throughout the cave
as we frantically attempted a
search. In my celerity, I failed
to dwell on just how utterly
impossible it would have been for
him to have vanished from our
sight in a matter of seconds,
especially in such a wide-open
space. I hadn't the faintest clue
as to how we were going to regroup
should we span the length of the

monumental fishbowl. "WAIT!" I loudly exclaimed. "Rally at the tunnel!" As we all gathered around the tunnel entrance, I gave the order to end our little unofficial search and continue the mission. "We will NOT leave Michael behind! When we return from this journey, Michael will either have followed us through, or will be awaiting our arrival at the cave-in." After some murmuring, the gaggle of disgruntled men conceded that this was the only logical move.

As we turned once more to enter the tunnel, I noticed a single set of boot prints leading into the maw of Bermuda Tunnel. As we approached, I saw that the prints seemed to cut off just prior to entering the tunnel. Puzzled by this, I peered into the maw of Bermuda Tunnel, and ordered my men to enter behind me.

CHAPTER 4

INTO THE MAW

"For since the creation of the world His invisible attributes, His eternal power and divine nature, having been clearly seen, being understood through what has been made, so that they are without excuse." -Romans 1:20

(Cont.) Entry 10: 11/08/2100
Henry insisted on leading the way, claiming it was because he had "lived a lot more" and that we "younger men have our whole lives ahead of us to take into account."

As we ventured in, the light around us seemed to bend or warp, almost as if we were approaching the epicenter of an infinitely dense gravitational singularity, a sort of impossible fragmentation of the fundamental laws of physics, and even time itself. Eventually, the walls of the cave darkened to pitch black, with only the occasional glistening of some indeterminable mineral upon passing by, mimicking the lifeless and starry void of space. I felt myself moving slower as I trailed directly behind Henry, who bravely ventured further still. I felt the previously theoretical, yet apparently tangible physical force of temporality affecting my body disproportionately. I had observed that some of my appendages felt as though they were submerged in a viscous fluid, whereas the rest of my body inexplicably felt more aerodynamic, as if suspended in a vacuum, perceiving this as a localized temporality differential. The other men accompanying me seemed to react to this as well, though not as profoundly. Strange noises began emanating from the approximate location where our rovers went dark. As we approached the area and the irritating noise measurably increased in decibels, our lighting systems began functioning once more, or perhaps whatever force was acting upon the surrounding light began to dissipate, or weaken. As our vision cleared, or whatever imperceptible and unnatural process occurred, the walls of the tunnel were illuminated, revealing hieroglyphic depictions of stick figures, alien in form. As we ventured further, the depictions warped into illustrations of these mysterious creatures. They depicted these beings building cities with incredible infrastructure, displaying the technological inclination of whoever, or whatever had produced these carvings. At this point, we were so enamored in what we'd witnessed so far, we were practically hypnotized. Even further still, the apparent hieroglyphics depicted the beings amassing a fleet of what were clearly meant to be massive space ships which were visiting other planets, including what was clearly meant to be Earth, Mercury, Venus, Pluto, Jupiter, and Mars. The ships themselves seemed to glisten within their rock-carved outlines, and appeared to be a strange, greyish-blue hue. "That can't be." I muttered. I yanked my geolometer from my pocket and took to analyzing what the material composition of those particular areas of the depictions were. It ran positive for the relatively newly discovered alloy. Absolutely beside myself, a range of emotions flooded my chest.

I'm still not exactly certain what I felt, nor what I was thinking throughout these subsequent events. Slowly approaching what we'd hoped against insurmountable odds was

the very end of the tunnel, a
flickering of blue light emanated
from the dark void ahead of me,
illuminating a great expanse
between me and whatever was
producing the mesmerizing flash.

I charged toward the light, and
upon reaching it I realized that
several other lights of various
colors and luminosities were
radiating incrementally from what
appeared to be an instrument panel
of some kind. There were no
obvious buttons, levers, or any
other interactive control
mechanisms. I began gently
pressing down on random lights in
hopes of soliciting some sort of
response or reaction from whatever
this panel presumably operated,
when the wall directly behind the
panel, which was the dead-end of
Bermuda Tunnel, began rumbling,
eventually splitting and crumbling
to dust. In a small pocket just
beyond the now defunct wall sat a

black, humanoid figure.
Absolutely beside myself in a mix
of unintelligible emotions, I sat
in silence behind the panel. 10
minutes had elapsed as I
anticipated some sort of movement
from the being, or the
acknowledgement of my existence at
the very least. It remained
perfectly still, with no
indication of any living thing in
the surrounding area at all
besides my crew and I. After
mustering enough courage, I walked
behind the control panel and
approached the unknown entity. I
noticed the darkness of it's
figure wasn't due to the absence
of light being reflected from it's
body, but the literal absence of
it's body. It appeared as though
the physical composition of the
creature was a void, a missing
chunk from the physical space in
which it occupied not devoid of
matter, but devoid of even the

physical plane of space itself,
a void of non-space isolated
entirely within the area which it
was occupying, if such a thing
were possible. It's nearly
impossible for me to properly
describe in written English what
the difference is between empty
space and "non-space," but it was
easily identifiable upon
witnessing it. It has long been
speculated that a third form of
existence, not just "nothing," but
the absolute antithesis of
"something" which can only "exist"
outside of the laws of physics,
could be present somewhere far
beyond the boundaries of space-
time, yet this theoretical
nothingness was undeniably right
there, localized entirely within
that little cave pocket. As I
cautiously approached the… thing,
time once again began warping, as
if it existed separately within
it, or somehow generated it's very

own temporal field. My men began
screaming my name, warning me to
back away, but as I further
approached the entity, their
voices slowed until they were
silent. The entity's form
surrounded me, enveloping me in
it's mysterious immaterial being.
In a surge of instinctive fear, I
shut my eyes tightly and smacked
my hands onto my helmet over where
my face was, hoping I wasn't
moments away from my own demise.

CHAPTER 5

AN ALIEN WORLD

"It's human nature to stretch, to go, to see, to understand. Exploration is not a choice really; it's an imperative." -Michael Collins, Apollo 11

(Cont.) Entry 10: 11/08/2100

In less than five seconds, behind the darkness of my eyelids, light began shining through. The distinct aroma of sulfur and sand wafted up to my nostrils. As my panic began to subside, I very slowly opened my eyes and peered through the gaps between my fingers. As I suspected, a vast ocean was before me, sporting a dim, blood-orange hue, waves lapping in the breeze as the sound of rushing wind blew past my ears intermittently. I immediately

surmised that this was an ocean
of liquid methane, or perhaps
liquid sulfur, though both of
these seemed utterly insane to
even consider. I knew that Titan,
a moon of Saturn, contains oceans
of liquid methane which typically
remain at around -292°F. Perhaps
the entity had brought me to such
a world, but if this were the
case, how could I survive such
temperatures, even in a US Space
Force grade suit, which aren't
rated for anything above 450°F,
nor below -250°F, with -246°F
being the lowest recorded extreme
temperature on Mars? Not to
mention, somehow I had nothing but
my uniform with me; no suit, no
equipment. The entire mission had
felt like a fever dream up to this
point, considering every
otherworldly occurrence I'd
previously thought to be
impossible utterly blindsiding me.
I even briefly questioned whether

my sanity could ever be regained
should I survive the ordeal.

Removing my hands from my face
and gazing upon the horizon, there
was no land in sight. Peering down
at my boots, I saw that I was
standing on a beach of burgundy
colored sand. Turning to look
behind me, I saw that the beach
stretched for miles, until it met
the horizon far into the distance.
The skies were blotched in patches
of violet and amethyst which
seemed to drown the planet's star
in a fluorescent haze. Realizing
that I was stranded on a foreign
planet, and possibly a foreign
realm of existence entirely, I
began sprinting in the opposite
direction of the ocean, hoping to
discover something lying just
beyond the alien horizon.
Eventually, off to my right, a
strange, scrawny figure emerged. I
immediately turned toward it and
bolted in that direction at speeds

that surely would've put an Olympic sprinter to shame. I stopped just short of the object. Panting, wheezing, and nearly dry heaving, I keeled over to catch my breath. Upon returning my gaze to the mysterious figure, I saw two blue, cylindrical objects, or sticks, more closely resembling coral skeletons than any earthly tree limb, fashioned together by some sort of grey twine, which seemed to be arranged in the shape of a cross, yet inverted. Immediately, Peter's cross came to mind. Old Catholic tradition states that Peter, when crucified by the Romans for refusing to renounce his faith in Christ, requested to be hanged on an upside down cross, stating that he was unworthy to die in the same manner as our Lord Jesus Christ, though the account is unverified by any Biblical or extrabiblical sources.

Assuming the cross was a marker for something, I began digging and rummaging through the sand, searching for anything that might lie below the cross. I eventually hit an air pocket. I pulled more sand up and out of the surrounding area, and realized the air pocket was emitting light. I didn't even stop to question how sand could levitate above an underground air pocket. With no regard for any potential hazards, I forced my entire arm through, and there was no end to the pit. Once I'd pushed enough sand aside, I poked my head through the opening, and was abruptly pulled through by some unknown force. I was falling from a sky identical to the one I'd just stood under moments prior. I slammed right back into the burgundy sand, returning to the foot of that presumably demonic cross. I had somehow fallen through the ground of this mysterious world, only to land in the exact spot I'd fallen from, entirely free of injury. It had occurred to me that the entity composed of "non-space" could've been demonic in nature rather than extraterrestrial. I stood up, collected myself, and began walking forward, in the direction opposite where the cross was facing. After what I estimated to be approximately eight miles of wandering with nothing visible as far as I could see, as I ascended a gradually inclined plane of sand, shapes began appearing on the horizon. I realized they had to have been man made, and began to swell with hope and excitement at the thought of finally encountering another human being.

CHAPTER 6

CITY OF DEVILS

"And the great dragon was thrown down, that ancient serpent, who is called the devil and Satan, the deceiver of the whole world—he was thrown down to the earth, and his angels were thrown down with him." -Revelation 12:9

(Cont.) Entry 10: 11/08/2100

As the foreign structures materialized over the brightly illuminated slope, it grew increasingly apparent to me that I was not viewing anything made by human hands, but a city of confounding architecture populated by a race of beings with scaly, green, iridescent skin and bulbous, black crescent eyes. They were considerably short in stature and humanoid in figure, and carried themselves with mannerisms that appeared to display a

perpetual sense of conceit, and
an air of superciliousness
parallel to human pride. I went
prone in the sand and kept leering
over the city. From simply
observing their behavior from
afar, their hauteur and pomposity
was so conspicuous that my
recognition of these traits
transcended our differing species.
Their puffed up chests and
aggressive gait were their most
glaring observable details. I
questioned what sort of taxonomic
classification these creatures
would be assigned should they be
studied by humanity. They were a
repugnant race, vile and
contemptible in appearance, which
seemed to subsist on the very sand
their civilization was forged
upon. Due to witnessing them
consume sand on a number of
occasions, I concluded through
deductive reasoning that these
creatures were likely silicon-

based life forms, or in layman's terms, rock people. All life on Earth is carbon-based, meaning carbon constitutes the core molecular structures of all living organisms. Carbon is essential to life as we know it, and the existence of life is thought to be impossible in it's absence. However, silicon is an element proposed to be a potential replacement for carbon in biochemistry, meaning there could be alien organisms who's molecular composition is silicon-based. Considering the biochemistry surrounding the conceptualization of silicon-based life is entirely theoretical, there was no way to know with absolute certainty what these being were unless I studied their physical properties extensively. Without my geolometer, I couldn't analyze the molecular makeup of the sand to get an idea of what compounds they

regularly consumed. I had a gut
feeling that these weren't
physical beings, that I'd either
been transported to some sort of
demonic spiritual realm, or that
these creatures were spiritual
beings visible from our material
plane of existence. There are no
scientific methods of measuring
the magnificent spiritual realm
that God has created simply due to
science's reliance on testing the
physically tangible
characteristics of it's subjects
to draw conclusions. The spiritual
realm is an unobservable,
intangible plane of existence
which is almost entirely
imperceptible to humanity in this
lifetime, with a number of
considerably rare and documented
exceptions. I simply could not
fully accept the idea that these
creatures physically existed, it
seemed contrary to everything
humanity had discovered regarding

the origin of mankind. The
account of creation and the Great
Flood as described in Genesis,
Sodom and Gomorra, the Tower of
Babel, the resurrection of Christ,
it had all been relatively proven
through diligent research in
various scientific fields. Nearly
all of mankind had complete faith
in the Word of God. I simply
couldn't reconcile this with the
existence of these creatures.

Their city was littered with
strange, baby blue, hook-like
structures that resembled small-
scale skyscrapers. They had no
vehicles or any means of
transportation aside from walking,
which they seemed to enjoy doing.
There were a multitude of
rectangular prism-shaped
structures much shorter in height
than their more colossal
counterparts littered about the
city, which seemed to be their
form of warehousing, or commercial

properties. The taller hook-like structures seemed to serve as both places of lodging, and some sort of executive business suites, perhaps communications office towers, or even a various mix of different industries similar to Earth's skyscrapers present in major cities such as New York and Chicago. The rest of their structures seemed to be residential dwellings.

The longer I would lie and monitor the beings, the more debauchery I would witness. I questioned whether their society had developed any laws, a code of ethics, or any sense of morality at the very least. I watched as one of them had killed five of his own kind within mere minutes, not far from the center of their city. He simply bludgeoned them with a blunt, heavily reflective, chrome-like tool resembling an oversized ball-peen hammer, and continued

about his business as if it were
an everyday occurrence, and I soon
realized that it truly was. I
wasn't nearly as mortified as I
likely should've been, considering
I knew nothing of their existence
other than the glimpse I'd taken
into their daily lives. I glanced
down at the analogue pocket watch
I kept in my suit pocket and
realized it had been a little over
seven hours since I'd been
transported to this eerie realm,
and four since I'd begun studying
the city. The planet's star was
beginning to sink below the
horizon, and dusk lit up the sky
in blindingly bright blue and red
hues that contrasted between the
clouds, in a similar manner to the
purple hue present in clouds
surrounding many sunsets back on
Earth. Like Earth, the planet was
obviously a part of a single-star
system, as it's host star was
clearly not gravitationally bound

to any other star, which would
be considered a binary star
system. Single star systems are
estimated to account for only 15%
of all stars in the known
universe, whereas 85% of all stars
exist in a binary star system or
star system consisting of three or
more stars. I believed the star to
be a blue giant, yet the skies
didn't exactly match up with the
theoretical result of a habitable
planet orbiting a blue giant,
which was puzzling. In the
hypothetical scenario of Earth
orbiting a blue giant or white
giant star, the atmosphere would
scatter the star's light in a
process known as Rayleigh
Scattering, which occurs when
light particles emitted from the
sun are entering Earth's
atmosphere and interact with
particles of a size up to 1/10th
their wavelength, which scatter
the light particles with no loss

of energy nor change in wavelength. This results in the bright blue coloration of Earth's skies observable during daylight hours. When applied to this scenario, this process would still scatter the stars light in such a way as to result in the skies remaining relatively the same color on this planet as they are on Earth while orbiting Sol, the yellow dwarf star that humanity has existed under since creation. I also felt the desire to discover precisely where in the star's habitable zone this planet resided in, as well as to map it's orbit, and perhaps the most fascinating aspect, discover what sort of atmospheric, meteorologic, or stellar variables were allowing for these presumably galactically scarce and incredibly vibrant shades of purple, red, and blue to permeate the skies. As the beauty of the dusk colors faded into a deep, purple night illuminated by stars, a planet of immense size appeared in the sky. It looked to be a gas giant, with several raging storms similar to those visible on the surface of Jupiter, which would indicate that the "planet" I was standing on was actually a sizable habitable satellite orbiting a gas giant within it's stellar system. I was on a moon. The night sky's deep amethyst hue intermingled with the gas giant's striking steel blue and cerulean glow to create a masterpiece of God's handiwork that would give Leonardo da Vinci a run for his money.

Though I'd grown weary in observing the beings, I hadn't grown parched or famished in the slightest. With the amount of information furiously swirling through my mind at any given moment, I hadn't once come close to realizing this, though even in retrospect it's quite puzzling. I spent a total of 4 of the planet's days, which seemed to be considerably shorter than Earth's days, lying in the sand, simply observing the society of creatures from afar. In this span of time, I'd witnessed countless murders, floggings, thefts, assaults, decapitations, dismemberments, among other such gruesome atrocities these beings inflicted on their own kind. It was truly a wonder to me that they could've cooperated long enough to construct their magnificent society, or even maintain it. Although I viewed approaching these things as a death sentence, I knew it was my only option. I finally pulled myself up from the sand, stretched my arms and legs out, and started calmly walking toward the city. As I did so, I spotted what appeared to be an airfield on the other side of the city, far beyond it's edge. There were several large, cigar-shaped and disc-shaped craft parked along the strip. As I approached further still, two of the craft took off from the runway and vanished, with no noise, no sonic boom, nothing. It was as if they'd either teleported or had become invisible, there was no trace of them whatsoever. It was startling, but I continued walking toward the city. As I came within view of a few of the creatures, none of them seemed to mind that I was an alien being approaching them on their own home satellite from the direction of a methane ocean that they were surely aware of. In fact, they didn't pay me any mind, not even glancing in my direction as I began walking throughout the city. Not once did they bother to interact with me or acknowledge my existence as I toured their city, witnessing some

of their strange and seemingly
ritualistic atrocities on a number
of occasions. As I wandered along
walking paths throughout the city,
I shot right past one of the
creatures when I noticed it's face
was peeling. A section of it's
iridescent skin at the base of
it's neck spidering up to it's
jawline was peeling and flaking,
as if it were molting. This
disturbed me greatly, though I
preemptively assumed it was the
literal result of the creature
molting it's scaly flesh. The next
few creatures I walked past were
in the same condition, yet at
varying stages. I took a few steps
backward until my back collided
with one of their skyscrapers. I
was startled by the sudden
realization that each of their
faces, while peeling at various
rates, were all simultaneously
molting, and the creatures that
were approaching the end of the

process were morphing into horrendous monstrosities. Their eyes were becoming human like, yet they were as black as night, entirely devoid of any life. Their skin was flaking off and becoming indescribably horrific, the mere sight of their ever-changing appearance was enough to induce a panic attack. Some of the creatures grew a varying number of horns, some grew bat-like wings, others grew goat-like facial features. Once my survival instincts caught up to my predicament, I bolted for the airfield, praying that whatever aircraft they had on site were capable of spaceflight.

There were no labels on any of the craft, no intelligible method of determining the intended use of any one craft. I discovered a latch on one of the cigar-shaped craft and pulled on it with all of the strength I could muster, finally prying the hatch open. As I entered the craft, it suddenly slammed shut behind me, leaving me in total darkness, dazed and disoriented.

CHAPTER 7

THE HAT MAN

""How you are fallen from heaven, O Day Star, son of Dawn! How you are cut down to the ground, you who laid the nations low! You said in your heart, 'I will ascend to heaven; above the stars of God I will set my throne on high; I will sit on the mount of assembly in the far reaches of the north; I will ascend above the heights of the clouds; I will make myself like the Most High.' But you are brought down to Sheol, to the far reaches of the pit." -Isaiah 14:12-15

(Cont.) Entry 10: 11/08/2100
I scanned around the ship frantically, unable to see anything but a dark void. It was deathly silent save for my own breath and rapid heartbeat. After what seemed like an eternity, a sudden flickering of light akin to the soft glow of a candle flame

began emanating from the opposite end of the ship. I approached the flame, and to my utter horror, in a leather chair, still as a statue, sat a man dressed in a grey suit, wearing a brimmed fedora or homburg style hat of the same color. He turned to face me with a patronizing grin smeared across his nearly human face which invoked the uncanny valley response in every fiber of my being. His eyes were too dark to be human, nearly pitch black with no visible sclera, with the rest of his face appearing relatively normal save for his condescending smile, which was unnaturally wide and menacing in the dim glow of the candle. What confounded me in that moment was not that this strange "man", presumably imitating a human being, was sitting before me displaying a revolting air of imperious, egotistical superiority. No, I had grown accustomed to this irritating behavior from my time with the iridescent beings. Rather, the chair had appeared out of thin air, and the man with it. I had turned my gaze to the light and followed it's glow, and the second I looked away before turning back to face the candle, he had appeared in that very instant, as if he intended to startle me.

He spoke to me in a deep, raspy, menacing tone: "Hello, John."

His voice seemed ancient and inhuman, it's difficult to describe, really. As startled as I was, I was growing weary of these psychologically torturous games. I'd automatically assumed this man was the same entity that had brought me to this foreign realm. "What do you want with me? Of what use am I to you? All of this time spent following a single man, for what?!" I rambled on, at a loss

for words and struggling to
formulate a coherent sentence.
After a brief period of silence
and a disturbing staring contest,
he then pulled himself from his
chair, standing up to a height of
at least 7 feet, and spoke once
more: "I know you human beings
quite well. I know what you are
searching for; meaning, knowledge,
purpose, understanding the origin
of existence as you know it. These
are more intertwined than you
realize. As surely as I stand
before you, I have the answer to
all of your wildest inquiries. I
have been to the outer reaches of
your galaxy and the very edge of
the cosmic web. I have witnessed
stars form and die. I have entered
the epicenter of black holes. I
have peered across eons of space
and time in observance of the very
fabric of existence. I can take
you there. I can reveal to you the

inner mechanisms of the
universe, if you so choose."
   I gave it a good minute or two
of thought. With no recourse, I
capitulated. "Alright, I suppose.
Show me." "We must shake on it."
He answered. "Take my hand." He
extended a long, lanky arm in my
direction. This was the first I'd
seen of his bare flesh; his hand
was dark and greyish in appearance
and seemed to have a sort of thin,
cellophane-like outer layer. I
reluctantly extended my hand to
shake his. Once I let go, blinding
light suddenly flooded my vision.
We were outdoors, on what appeared
to be earth upon first glance.
There were green, luscious forests
surrounding the grassy field we
stood upon. My body felt as though
it were being vacuumed toward the
ground, indicating an obvious
increase in gravity. "Where is
this?!" I pressed. "We are

standing on the surface of Kepler 452b, an exoplanet inhabited by some of the most commonly occurring forms of carbon based life. Be warned, this planet is 60% larger than Earth, so as a result, it's gravitational force is roughly doubled. You're currently experiencing a day in the life of a 400lb man, John. We are 1,800 light years, or approximately 9,000,000 years worth of modern space travel time from Earth. On this planet, life exists in abundance and roams freely about, just as it does on Earth. Your planet is not unique, nor is it special in any regard. It is simply a product of the initial expansion of the original singularity which created your universe." He explained this as if he were attempting to sway my worldview. Whatever his motives were, it was clear to me that he desperately wanted me to believe what he was telling me. "I really have to question why you're putting this much effort into revealing this to one man. I'm hesitant to even consider what you're implying. You claim that life exists in abundance throughout the universe, yet planets orbiting within the habitable zones of their stars only account for an estimated 0.9% of all planets confirmed to exist. It's simply not logical." I retorted. "Ah, but do you trust your scientists? Have they not made extravagant claims in the past? They've previously made the outlandish claim that smoking is healthy for young children to engage in, do you find this to be sensible? How much of a grasp do you have on the true inner workings of the bureaucracy of your organization? Do you truly believe you know everything?" He once again rambled, attempting to discredit my organization and the people I've worked with for decades. "If you're attempting to gain my trust or convince me that my life is a lie, you're doing a very poor job. The men I work with are not corrupt scumbags, and they're not being paid off by some large industrial complex to push harmful products. We're attempting to colonize a planet, how would that even affect our work? You make no sense." I replied, my anger gradually welling up in my chest. "Perhaps this will change your mind." With the snap of the man's fingers, we appeared before the strange civilization of iridescent beings once more, however, we were peering into their distant past, when they were first discovering fire. The man then snapped his fingers, and time moved around us at unfathomable speeds, finally slowing to a usual pace, revealing a few of the beings forging weapons from various metals they'd sifted from the sand. Under what looked to be a tin roof, at a station reminiscent of a blacksmith's workshop, primitive, silvery hammers, knives, and swords were being pulled from kilns and beaten into shape. They were clearly advancing as a society from their previous discovery of fire, presumably thousands of years into their past. I knew what the hat man was trying to imply; that not only had life been abundant throughout the universe since the beginning of time, but that it's means of existing hinged upon evolution, which had been disproven many decades before. I knew that he was pushing a false narrative to persuade me of something, and my suspicions were aroused. I knew it had something to do with convincing the rest of humanity of some secular narrative of existence, and I wasn't buying what this strange man was selling. Everything he was demonstrating could've been an illusion for all I knew, and it was antithetical to the many scientific leaps and bounds we'd made, leaving me convinced that he had ulterior motives.

The man then waved his hand, and in another display of temporal manipulation, time once again leapt forward, this time settling right on the completed city that I'd visited prior to my encounter with the hat man. "You see? This technological and evolutionary progression is nearly as abundant as hydrogen in the universe. Many planets that you believe to reside far away from their star's habitable zones are indeed habitable. You're simply not searching with the right frame of mind. Let me reveal something else to you, this is sure to shock you

97

to your core. Another handshake, John?" Questioning why I had to comply with his childish handshake ritual for his abilities to function, I once again shook his hand, and upon retracting mine, we were standing stationary in the atmosphere of a planet. Looking up, the sky was blue and strikingly similar to Earth. My boots dangling in the sky, looking below, I saw large clouds of dust swirling in patterns like ice cream. I knew immediately that we were hovering over the raging storms of a gas giant, and Jupiter came to mind. "Yes, John, this is Jupiter's upper atmosphere." He quipped, as if he were reading my mind. "This particular Jovian atmospheric layer is perfectly habitable, and hosts city-sized, jellyfish-like creatures capable of maintaining neutral buoyancy via internal organs acting as gas pockets that continuously fill with, and release filtered, pure hydrogen which is slightly less dense than the surrounding atmosphere, which is mixed with approximately 10% helium. There are microscopic Jovian life forms floating about that these creatures filter feed on for their sustenance. As I've already explained to you, John, the galaxy is teeming with decillions of incomprehensibly alien life forms, and the universe as a whole with decillions of centillions. You and your civilization are blind to the reality of the true abundance of life." I continued eyeing the city-sized beasts as he spoke. They peaceably moved about the atmosphere, swaying across the upper layers while a storm of over 400mph was raging just below them. With the snap of the hat man's fingers, in the blink of an eye, I was once again standing on those

burgundy shores, staring out
over oceans of liquid methane as
the blue giant star rose over the
edge of the horizon.

CHAPTER 8

UNMASKED

"You are of your father the devil, and your will is to do your father's desires. He was a murderer from the beginning, and does not stand in the truth, because there is no truth in him. When he lies, he speaks out of his own character, for he is a liar and the father of lies." -John 8:44

(Cont.) Entry 10: 11/08/2100
As we "stood" over the magnificent Jovian world, the hat man turned to me, his eyes betraying an inkling of amusement and glee, his expression appeared remorseful, but forced. "There is something I've withheld from you, John. Not to worry, it isn't pertinent to our discussion, however, I am what you'd refer to as the 'evil' one." He visibly struggled to contain his grin as it began to break out across his

face. "You're telling me…
you're…" "Yes, I go by many a
name. El diablo. Le diable. Der
teufel. The tempter. Allah. The
devil. The god of this age.
Beelzebul. Baal. Molech. Belial.
The father of lies. Lucifer. I'm
most commonly referred to as satan
by your species, though I'm afraid
you have my motives confused. You
humans commonly lock me into the
wrong side of history when
considering the cosmic war between
good and evil, but I'm afraid the
truth is much more nuanced than
you people care to admit. You
cannot simply judge each of my
actions as atrocious without first
considering the Biblical narrative
from my perspective. For one, the
majority of what your precious
Bible claims is historical fact is
errant falsehood. The creation
account in Genesis is laughable at
best, clearly evolution is the
driving force behind the existence

of all matter in the universe, and can be broken down into both cosmic and biological evolution, and this is only the tip of the iceberg."

"What you've failed to account for," I immediately began. "The Biblical narrative of creation has already been proven beyond a shadow of a doubt by insurmountable archeologic and geologic evidence. The inerrancy of the Biblical narrative as a whole has been proven to be bullet-proof. The archeological evidence supporting the Gospel account of the life of Christ alone is mind boggling. Peter's house, the pool of Siloam, the pool of Bethesda, Jacob's well, Golgotha, Ciaphas' house. Not to mention the remains of Sodom & Gomorrah which contain the purest sulfur balls on Earth, the many contemporary philosophers and historians hostile to the narrative such as Josephus, who confirmed the various details of Christ's life found in the Gospels, the layer of sediment present in soil which confirms the Biblical flood, wild radiocarbon-14 dating inaccuracies and the impossibility of dating inorganic fossils, the foolishness of uniformitarianism, the lack of transitional forms, the deceit of secular institutions such as the Smithsonian over the previous two centuries to push fabricated humanoid "missing links" to maintain their precious facade of the ostensibly apodeictic evolutionary narrative, I could go on for years! You lie through your teeth, satan! Your arguments are identical to the abysmal mainstream secular ideology of the 2030's! You planted this idiocy in the minds of our forefathers, you truly are the father of lies!" My indignation steadily grew into a blinding, fiery rage. He began once again, seemingly moving on from his failed assertions.

"It may be true that I was cast from the highest heaven, but only because I wished for my acquaintances and I to have equal authority with God in heavenly matters, which I would deem to be a reasonable desire as His highest angel. I've wandered the universe for many thousands of years, all I've done is attempt to elevate humanity to a position equal with their Creator. What crime have I committed? It is humanity, not God Himself, that has tainted and corrupted the Biblical narrative throughout eons of time, rewriting history and obscuring my true role in your story. Every book of every Bible is corrupted beyond measure, there is no archeological evidence to the contrary."

"Nonsense!" I chuckled at his pathetic stupidity. "You've hated mankind from the beginning, because he is created in the image and likeness of God, and no matter what power you hold, you'll never attain such favorability from God. Back to the notion of the Biblical narrative being hogwash, as I previously mentioned and you conveniently failed to address, there is archeological and historical evidence backing every recorded event in the Bible in some fashion. The Dead Sea Scrolls were found between 1946-1956 in the Qumran Caves near Ein Feshkha on the Northern Shore of the Dead Sea. They contain nearly the entire Old Testament and are over 99% identical to modern Bible translations. It is verifiably factual that no changes have been made to the Biblical narrative since the time of Christ. There are other smaller fragments of other books of the Bible from 2,700 years ago, dating back to

the time of the Kingdom of Judah
when Solomon's Temple still stood
as a dwelling place for the Lord.
The fragment reads:
    'The Lord bless you and keep
    you; the Lord make his face
    shine on you and be gracious to
    you; the Lord turn his face
    toward you and give you peace.'
It's from Numbers 6:24-26, and
reads just as our modern
translations do over 2,700 years
later. There is not one evidential
indication of any changes made to
the Biblical narrative,
intentional or otherwise. As I've
mentioned previously, you are a
liar and the father of it. You, a
roaring lion, believe you can
devour me and the rest humanity at
a point in history when your world
influence is but a bloated corpse.
It's sad and pathetic."
    He stood staring through me for
a bit, as if he were concocting
some foolhardy reply. That same

mischievous grin spread across his evil face once more as he began to speak; "Now, I've already shown you a minute fraction the incredible forms of life that exist on other planets. Why then, do you suppose, that God created this universe over 13,000,000,000 years ago, only to leave you and all other extant forms of life? To allow you to change and evolve throughout the eons, hopeless and directionless, with no divine intervention? Do you really believe that He cares for *you, you yourself, you* personally when there are centillions of planets hosting sentient life that all suffer continuously just as you do? If Yahweh exists, and Yeshua is your Messiah as you believe, and both are omnipotent and omniscient, then why is it that hundreds of children die of childhood cancer per day? You seem deluded, John. I'm only guiding

you back to the light of
rationality and reason." He
finished, his face expressing a
smug demeanor, clearly indicating
he truly believed he'd won.
Unfortunately for him, I'd had
this discussion with the very few
atheists that still remain on
Earth dozens of times, though in a
much more polite and respectful
manner. However, I refused to be
cordial with the one for whom hell
itself was prepared. As swiftly as
the evil one's chest swelled with
confidence that he'd won the
battle, in the name of the Lord, I
opened my mouth and I cut him down
to Gehenna.

"Where to start? For one, I
don't accept a single vision
you've implanted into my mind as
factual or legitimate. I don't
believe for a second that there is
any other sentient life capable of
reasoning or comprehending
anything beyond their own

instinctual drives. What you've presented is verifiably false. We are the only sentient life in existence, and our planet is very likely to be the only one in the universe which hosts life, and is likely the only planet on which life is even sustainable, for that matter. Your baseless claims are futile in shifting what I know to be true. God demonstrated His love for us in stepping down from His heavenly throne to live a life of suffering, only to be nailed to a wooden cross and die an unbearably painful death. During his crucifixion, He had ample power and opportunity to call upon a legion of angels to stop the torment, yet His love for each individual human being is what kept Him there until His work was finished. He has conquered sin and death and has opened the gates of heaven, and yet you continue laboring to damn the souls of

God's people in vain. He has shown His love for us in His death and resurrection, you have shown nothing but the very origin of hatred and contempt for mankind's existence." I concluded.

"You still haven't answered one of my fundamental inquiries into the basis of your faith, John." The evil one began once more. "Why is it that God, in His infinite glory, power and wisdom, allows children to starve or contract various diseases and forms of cancer? Why is it that God allows kingdoms and empires faithful to Him to fall, and others who are arguably more depraved than Sodom and are more immersed in satisfying their own fleshly desires than Gomorra, to flourish? Why do evil men of unrepentant hearts with unregenerate lives given honor and authority on Earth, while men of devout piety and austere sanctitude reduced to

111

suffering and misery? Should
such an allegedly merciful
Shepherd not provide much-needed
relief to His flock? Why have
famine, war, disease, and the like
been so globally persistent
throughout preceding eras of human
history?" I moved my lips in
preparation for a response, but he
cut me off before I could speak.
"Or could the answer be simple?
Occam's razor tells us that the
simplest explanation is likely to
be the correct one, and I argue
that your God did not create you,
nor anything in the observable
universe, but that He simply
placed an infinitely dense
singularity into the void of this
particular plane of existence upon
which He had burdened with a
particular set of parameters which
currently govern it's operation,
allowing the singularity to expand
outward and develop undisturbed
through the carefully constructed

laws of cosmic and biological evolution, which are the prerequisites of your very existence, into the cosmic web of matter and energy you dwell in today. Humanity is so insignificant to the universe as a whole that it cannot even be regarded as a speck in it's eye. Perhaps God is blissfully unaware of your existence." He finished, and I responded with the refutations I'd already carefully constructed in my mind while listening.

CHAPTER 9

REFUTING DECEPTION

"Do not be deceived: God is not mocked, for whatever one sows, that will he also reap. For the one who sows to his own flesh will from the flesh reap corruption, but the one who sows to the Spirit will from the Spirit reap eternal life."
-Galatians 6:7-8

(Cont.) Entry 10: 11/08/2100
"Your argument seems to stem from a presupposition that many mistakenly have, that God is not a God of justice, only of love and mercy. God is certainly the originator and progenitor of love and mercy, but also of justice and fairness. When sin entered into the world and mankind had fallen from their previously perfect and

sinless state, God cursed the ground, forcing Adam and his descendants to toil and labor for their food. *"To Adam he said, "Because you listened to your wife and ate fruit from the tree about which I commanded you, 'You must not eat from it,' 'Cursed is the ground because of you; through painful toil you will eat food from it all the days of your life. It will produce thorns and thistles for you, and you will eat the plants of the field. By the sweat of your brow you will eat your food until you return to the ground, since from it you were taken; for dust you are and to dust you will return.'"*

(Genesis 3:17-19)

When God had first confronted Adam and Eve, he said to Eve in Genesis 3:16; *"To the woman he said, 'I will make your pains in childbearing very severe; with*

painful labor you will give
birth to children. Your desire
will be for your husband, and he
will rule over you.'"

From this day, suffering had
entered into the world, along with
sin and death, and mankind was
further susceptible to *YOUR*
deception, satan! Suffering is,
and has always been a byproduct of
sin, and sin itself being a
byproduct of mankind searching for
satisfaction in futile things. To
quote C.S. Lewis; '*Human history*
is the long, terrible story of man
trying to find something other
than God which will make him
happy.' It is not the will of God
that anyone should suffer or
perish, but that all would come to
a fullness in knowledge of Christ
and His glory and be sanctified
for His approaching day. How is
it, you ask, that God allows the
suffering of mankind? To kill two

birds with one stone, I'll tack on another question. Why does God send human beings to hell? God does not send any man to hell. If he goes, it is of his own volition. (Rev. 21:8) God has given all mankind what is necessary for salvation, from the day of Christ's resurrection and onward it has been a choice to be cast into hell. You enter hell by making the conscious decision to reject Christ, His sacrifice, and His life that He has given freely to you, and He will honor your decision, made in your own free will, by separating you from Himself eternally. As to the point of why God would allow suffering? He does not. Mankind is responsible for his own suffering by the choices he makes through his own free will. It's not as if it is exclusively every man who has committed some form of sin that is subject to suffering and

all other human beings are
exempt, all have come under the
righteous judgement of God for the
sins of mankind and are the
recipients of the conditions of
our fallen state. Christ would
have been perfectly justified in
destroying all of mankind and
casting each of them into hell at
any point from creation to the
present moment, it is His love,
patience and long-suffering that
prevents this. This insufferable
moral posturing over God Himself
and what He knows to be right,
attempting to elevate oneself
above He who created all, is the
very idiotic act which sank
humanity into the Era Of Decline,
a period of moral, cultural, and
technological reversion which
lasted from 2015-2035, not to
mention a successful revolution in
the United States as an attempt to
combat such societal decay. By
early 2035, archeology and geology

had proven the historicity of the Biblical narrative, and the disastrous consequences of the core tenants of the western left-wing cult drove the world into an all out revolutionary war, followed by a rebellious Christian Renaissance and Revival, dismantling any foothold gender ideology had in the American social sphere, sparking a worldwide post-revolution reclamation of western culture, society, and political and educational institutions that has lasted up to the present time. It is said by historians to be the most prosperous and productive era in the entirety of human history. Is not your main inquiry concerning why it is that God would allow suffering? I would ask you why it is that God allows joy and prosperity in a world saturated in human evil and depravity? Is it not the righteous judgement of God that all should give account for their evil deeds? And has He not rescued us from our deserved fate in spite of our own rejection, rebellion and stupidity? To ask even for what He has already done to secure our seat at His table in glory is unthinkable. To answer your question, all have sinned, and all have fallen short of the glory of God. (Romans 3:23) Any fate short of hellfire for any human being is a testament to the mercy of the Almighty."

As I finished my refutation, that same demonic grin stretched across the face of the evil one once more.

"I'm afraid I have more yet unanswered inquiries concerning the nature of your faith. There are as many as 45,000 denominations of Christianity globally, each of which claim to represent the true body of Christ, and each of which claim to present every Biblical doctrine in absolute truth and clarity. These denominations can be reduced to six main taxonomic classifications; the Church of the East, Oriental Orthodoxy, Roman Catholicism, Protestantism, and Restorationism. Each of these main classifications are at odds with each other concerning fundamental Christian doctrines such as papal supremacy and primacy, ecumenism, the true divine nature of Christ, apostolic succession, conciliarity, and even the very nature of salvation and the means of obtaining it. There are many internal disputes even within these 45,000 or so denominations as to whether or not ecumenical councils, or church leadership in general hold any authentic spiritual authority on which to base any particular claims they make or doctrines they adhere to.

Many also argue over whether Christ was in fact God in the flesh, as well as the doctrine of modalism, or modalist monarchism, the idea that the Father, the Son, and the Holy Spirit are three "modes" of God which He can appear in at any time He chooses, essentially that The Father, the Son, and the Holy Spirit are all three "modes" of God. This is widely regarded as a heretical doctrine by mainstream Christianity, yet widely remains a point of contention. Aside from an inability to agree on these important points, many also argue over whether praying to, or as they would refer to it, asking Mary and the canonized saints of catholicism for intercession is biblical. The list of seemingly eternal doctrinal fractures debates is without end.

Is it not reasonable to assume then, that if Christianity is so fractured beyond recognition, perhaps the foundational premises of the religion itself are fundamentally flawed? Could these disagreements stem from an issue rooted much deeper in the core of spirituality itself? Could spirituality itself only be a byproduct of the evolutionary processes which implanted this tendency to develop religions into the human psyche, forcing mankind to structure their societies in this style of leadership to ensure their own survival? Could it be that man is spiritual simply because the natural evolutionary processes, by an impeccably minute chance rooted in necessity, have made it so?" He finished speaking, and I began refuting his materialistic and pharisaical arguments once more. "There is no particular denomination that can be pinpointed as particularly correct in their theology. It is true that minor theological differences among congregants of a certain denomination have resulted in fracturing and the creation of many new denominations of Christianity historically, but that doesn't prevent either side from entering into the glory of God. The body of Christ consists of His true believers, those who truly obey His Word and run the race of the Christian life as God has commanded them. The true body of Christ consists of many appendages, joints, heads, feet, arms, legs. It consists of many millions from all denominations that have true faith in Christ and believe His gospel. Your denomination doesn't determine your salvation, God does. His requisites are to place your faith in His one and only Son who stepped down from His throne of glory and sacrificed His life, bearing the burden of the world's sin, so we might dwell with Him. Therefore, all who follow the true Christ, the One True God, are members of His body, regardless of religious affiliations. In this knowledge it becomes apparent just how trivial denominations truly are. I believe it would be prudent to quote C.S. Lewis in his collection of speeches he gave on live radio broadcasts in the 1940's titled *Mere Christianity*. The beginning is in reference to C.S. Lewis' desire for the reader to not regard "Mere Christianity" as a replacement to any particular Christian denomination, explaining just what his work is intended to do:

"*It is more like a hall out of which doors open into several rooms.*

But it is in the rooms, not in the hall, that there are fires and chairs and meals. The hall is a place to wait in, a place from which to try the various doors, not a place to live in. For that purpose the worst of the rooms is, I think, preferable. It is true that some people may find they have to wait in the hall for a considerable time, while others feel certain almost at once which door they must knock at. I do not know why there is this difference, but I am sure God keeps no one waiting unless He sees that it is good for him to wait. You must keep on praying for light: and, of course, even in the hall, you must begin trying to obey the rules which are common to the whole house. When you have reached your own room, be kind to those who have chosen different doors and to those who are still in the hall. If they are wrong they need your prayers all the more; and if they are your enemies, then you are under orders to pray for them. That is one of the rules common to *the whole house."*

There is no one Christian denomination that is correct, simply because it is not in the denomination that a man be a true Christian, but faith in Christ. Strife within denominations is heavily warned against by Paul, the apostle to the gentiles. Romans 16:17-18 states; *"I appeal to you, brothers, to watch out for those who cause divisions and create obstacles contrary to the doctrine that you have been taught; avoid them. For such persons do not serve our Lord Christ, but their own appetites, and by smooth talk and flattery they deceive the hearts of the naive."*

This is a general appeal to the people of God to avoid those who cause drama and stir up arguments within the body of Christ, but this can also be applied to those

who start arguments over
doctrinal differences for no good
reason. It is true that there are
men and women of God in all
denominations of Christianity that
truly follow Christ, though there
are many denominations that deny
the true Christ, worship other
gods, exalt man in the place of
God, or compromise on sin, and
their differences are
irreconcilable with the true body
of Christ. By and large, however,
the many doctrinal disputes
between denominations are trivial
at best, and serve no purpose
other than distracting from
bearing the fruit of the Holy
Spirit of God."

Seemingly switching tactics on a
whim, the evil one extended his
hand, beckoning me to shake it for
another galactic excursion. "I
think you'd simply better
transport us, I'm not shaking your
hand." I said defiantly. "Very

well." He responded, before snapping his fingers and instantly transporting us to the vacuum of space. In spite of this lack of atmosphere, I was somehow able to breathe normally. I was staring off into a cross section of a galaxy that I presumed to be the Andromeda considering it's barred spiral appearance, when the hat man tapped my shoulder from behind me. I placed my hand on his shoulder to spin myself around in the vacuum of space to face his direction, only to find that he'd nearly brought me within reach of a blue giant star. It's bright, blinding rays were akin to staring into an LED light. The "hat man" motioned his hand, apparently somehow adjusting my eyesight as the star dimmed to a glow, and I was suddenly able to perceive it's finer details. Large plumes of burning plasma bellowed up from below the star's surface. It was

surrounded by a few visible
planets suspended around the star
in orbit which were almost small
enough to be mistaken as far
distant stars, not much else about
them was discernible. The evil one
somehow caused us to rapidly orbit
the star until we wore facing it's
opposite side, which revealed a
long, stringy jet of blue plasma
extending out from it's surface
until it came to a sharp point
around a pitch-black sphere. The
sphere seemed to be ejecting
continuous streams of white hot
matter in two opposite directions,
while some of the blue matter was
breaking down and orbiting the
sphere. I immediately knew what I
was witnessing. "So you've finally
come to realize, John..." The hat
man began. "Just how insignificant
your world, and the universe as a
whole, truly is in the grand
scheme of things. Stars are born,
and eventually die. Even this

black hole that is actively consuming this blue giant will eventually fizzle out due to the emission of Hawking radiation. All things have an expected and calculable end, John, even life as you know it. In the end, all things will cease to be, leaving nothing but the faint echos of what mankind once was on dead planets which managed to escape the all-consuming death of their star. Some would consider this revelation a sort of existential or cosmic horror, I say it's simply the way of the world, the truth that mankind has been searching for so desperately for so long. You simply cannot allow your emotions to dictate your beliefs as do these dreaded 'antiquated' authoritarian leftists which you hold in such a low regard.

Was Christianity not considered antiquated or archaic at the height of their regime? And yet by 2038, Christian warriors from all corners of the west gathered against their enemies to water the tree of liberty and restore peace and freedom to the nation which their forefathers had settled and built, or so they believed. The truth, however, is self-evident. You've been deceived. Christian superstition has held humanity back from any meaningful scientific advancements for centuries." He finished, that same devilish smirk plastered across his face indicating he was well pleased with the lies he'd just spewed. I took a moment to respond, wondering just why it was that the evil one refused to leave me be. I considered what Christ had done in the wilderness to refute satan. He didn't continuously rely on logical arguments rooted in secular scientific disciplines, but rather, He responded to every temptation with the one authority that even satan himself recognized; The Word of God. Christ had thrown verse after verse of scripture in the face of the devil to refute his falsehoods. Once I'd considered this, I realized my tactics were only allowing me to refute the evil one's stupidity as quickly as he could spew it, yet would not put an end to his attempt at reclaiming the world any time soon. I knew his ultimate goal in this endeavor was to supplant my worldview so I would report what I've seen back to NASA and skew the whole world's Christian faith toward an atheist viewpoint, something I knew God was strengthening me to prevent. I decided to respond in a similar manner as Christ did. "It is true that there is nothing new under the sun. Ecclesiastes 1:1-11;

" 'Meaningless! Meaningless!'
says the Teacher.
'Utterly meaningless!
Everything is meaningless.'
What do people gain from all their
labors at which they toil under
the sun? Generations come and
generations go, but the earth
remains forever. The sun rises and
the sun sets, and hurries back to
where it rises. The wind blows to
the south and turns to the north;
round and round it goes, ever
returning on its course. All
streams flow into the sea, yet the
sea is never full. To the place
the streams come from, there they
return again. All things are
wearisome, more than one can say.
The eye never has enough of
seeing, nor the ear its fill of
hearing. What has been will be
again, what has been done will be
done again; there is nothing new
under the sun. Is there anything
of which one can say, 'Look! This

*is something new'? It was here
already, long ago; it was here
before our time. No one remembers
the former generations, and even
those yet to come will not be
remembered by those who follow
them."*

In fact, all things continue as
they were since the beginning of
creation, and will until the
appointed time of Christ's return,
the last hour. 2 Peter 3:4; *"They
will say, 'Where is the promise of
his coming? For ever since the
fathers fell asleep, all things
are continuing as they were from
the beginning of creation.'"* All
things will continue in the cycles
God has designated for them, and
there is no new thing under the
sun. God has created all things
for the benefit of Him, this
includes the infinite expanse of
galaxies throughout the cosmic web
spanning tens of billions of
lightyears. Colossians 1:16; *"For*

by him all things were created, in heaven and on earth, visible and invisible, whether thrones or dominions or rulers or authorities —all things were created through him and for him." Out of all creation we are the only things created in His image. Genesis 1:26:28; *"Then God said, 'Let us make man[h] in our image, after our likeness. And let them have dominion over the fish of the sea and over the birds of the heavens and over the livestock and over all the earth and over every creeping thing that creeps on the earth.'*

So God created man in his own image, in the image of God he created him; male and female he created them. And God blessed them. And God said to them, 'Be fruitful and multiply and fill the earth and subdue it, and have dominion over the fish of the sea and over the birds of the heavens

and over every living thing that
moves on the earth.' God also hand
crafts every human being with love
and intent. Psalm 139:13-16; "For
you created my inmost being;
     you knit me together in my
mother's womb.
     I praise you because I am
fearfully and wonderfully made;
     your works are wonderful,
     I know that full well.
     My frame was not hidden from you
     when I was made in the secret
place, when I was woven together
in the depths of the earth. Your
eyes saw my unformed body; all the
days ordained for me were written
in your book before one of them
came to be."
God loved each of us with an
everlasting love, every human
being who has ever lived was
formed by the very hand of God.
God loves each of His people with
an incomprehensible and
indescribable love, which is

exactly why I cannot allow you to infect the minds of God's people, belial! You Deceiver! You've been a liar since the beginning, and God willing He will soon cast you from my presence!"

I finished, before I began calling on the name of Christ, the Son of the Most High God to drive out the evil one. As I continue praying, I began feeling the presence of God, so overwhelmingly powerful that I truly believed it would destroy me. I was suddenly blinded by a white burst of light so powerful that neither my eyelids, nor even my arms stood any chance of protecting my eyes. I heard the evil on screaming and writhing in agony as he cursed and insulted God. Despite putting up a fight, he clearly understood that it was no use. I felt myself slipping into a deep sleep as the light slowly dimmed to a soft glow, and I lost consciousness.

CHAPTER 10

THE RETURN

"You believe that God is one; you do well. Even the demons believe—and shudder!" James 2:19

(Cont.) Entry 10: 11/08/2100
When I awoke, I stood up to survey my surroundings before noticing a familiar incremental flashing of lights emanating from behind a wall of some sort. I was in the space behind the control panel, which looked to be a short steel wall or table from behind. I was still reeling from all that had happened, and the confirmation that our faith in Christ is well-placed. I was still wearing my full suit, and had plenty of remaining oxygen. As I began to exit the tunnel, I realized my crew was nowhere to be found. I cautiously made my way past the

hieroglyphics, only to find that
that particular area of the tunnel
was no longer warping light and
bending the surrounding temporal
field. I figured a lot of the
strange events I'd witnessed were
simply illusions generated by
demonic beings to further the evil
one's agenda. I took this further
and deduced that the technology
left in the main cavern, such as
the strange alloy, was only
fabricated by some sort of demonic
entity to give the appearance that
some alien beings had landed in
MOSS Cavern at some distant point
in the past and left behind behind
advanced technology. We were still
able to utilize the technology
despite the nefarious ulterior
motives of those who'd left it.

I exited the tunnel to find the
crew resting on the ground with
their equipment scattered about.
They were each sleeping with their

heads on their bags. There were
perhaps hundreds of empty MRE
(Meal Ready to Eat) bags as well.
I feared they'd somehow starved in
the short time I was away, though
we had brought enough food and
water to last several months in
the event of a cave-in. I
cautiously approached them, and
peered into Nehemiah's visor. I
saw his eyes were shut and he
wasn't moving, so I read the meter
on his oxygen supply, which
indicated his supply was at 96%
capacity and was being consumed at
a typical rate. I tapped his
shoulder, and he instantly shot up
from his resting position and
looked me dead in the helmet.
"JOHN!" He shouted as loud as
possible. "JOHN IS BACK! GET UP!
HE'S HERE!" The rest of the crew
awoke from the slumber and were
less-than-polite about telling
Nehemiah to quiet down. I saw that
Michael was once again among the

group. "We thought you were killed by that creature." Henry began explaining. "We've been waiting here to die for over two months now!" "Why? Could you not recall the rovers on the opposite end of the cave-in?" I asked with a puzzled look on my face. "You're the only one who knows the master access code for the rovers' remote software. We tried digging through the rubble, but but it only exacerbated the situation by thickening the mess." "So you've been stuck here. I'm sorry fellas. Do you have enough food and water?" I asked. "Enough to last several more months." Henry replied. "I've been the temporary 'captain' of this crew for the past few months. Now that you've returned to us safely, Dr. Duncan, I'd like to formally relinquish my command back to you." "I thank you for that, Henry. Did Jeremy give you any issues?" I inquired as I began remotely reactivating the now dormant rovers and directing them to clear the cave-in to reach us. "I had to put him in his place a few times, he's a cocky one." "Insubordinate and endangering." I muttered. "Say, why don't you finish setting up those rovers and have a freeze-dried ice cream sandwich and MRE dinner with us while you explain what exactly happened over the two whole months you were missing?" Henry proposed. "Sure. Was I actually missing from the cave, or just unconscious?" "No, you were gone. Not a trace of you left anywhere. We searched behind that control doohickey and throughout the tunnel… nothing. Every trace of anything abnormal or supernatural vanished right along with you, John. Over the few months we spent in this cave, we'd resigned ourselves to our inevitable deaths, hoping you'd somehow return to us unharmed.

143

We've rationed out supplies
despite having nearly a years
worth, we knew it would be wise to
stretch them. Now that our escape
is guaranteed, we can indulge a
little. Come have a celebratory
feast with us and tell us what you
saw, I'm dying to know."

Once I'd explained the
previously recorded events, I fell
silent as the crew processed what
I'd just shared with them.
Nehemiah then stood to his feet.
"Brothers," he began. "The Lord
has given us a great blessing in
facilitating the safe return of
our commander, thereby saving our
wretched lives from a gruesome
fate. Let us give thanks in
prayer, and ask that the Lord our
God continue to guide us in all of
our endeavors!" With that, we all
stood to our knees and began
praying. Once finished, I decided
to check my geolometer. We still
had several hours to spend in the

cave, waiting for the rovers to clear the remaining dirt and stones. I directed my men to reenter the tunnel and gather any artifacts and supplies we could. While they were busy chiseling away at the hieroglyphs, I returned to the control panel to examine it, but the area in which I'd first encountered the hat man had vanished, with the wall replaced. Curious, I approached the panel and examined it for any screws or removable parts, but it was entirely seamless, as if it were forged from a solid chunk of metal. I decided to attempt to cut my way into it, only to discover there were dozens of wires hooked to various strange computer boards scattered throughout the contraption. I pushed every button and pulled every lever in an attempt to elicit a response, but nothing. I simply replaced the sheet of metal I'd removed from

the panel and left. Once my men
had reanalyzed the material
composing the hieroglyphic
spacecraft, they concluded it was
composed of the same martian soil
as the rest of them and was
somehow no longer composed of the
alloy, which was puzzling to say
the least. They carefully
extricated four several foot long
panels of hieroglyphic depictions
from the tunnel walls to drag back
to the MOSS for further analysis.
After bonding over freeze-dried
military rations for hours on end,
the rovers finally removed the
last of the debris. We swiftly
packed our gear and exited the
cavern, finally surfacing after
what felt like an eternal stent in
the depths of Gehenna. Stepping
onto that pod for our return trip
was the most relieving feeling
I've ever experienced. It felt as
though I'd returned from the
gallows after being sentenced to

hang. We threw our gear in, docked the rovers, and jumped aboard the pod. Once we were safely aboard and on our way to the station, I decided to attempt to transmit a radio message to Dr. Brogg to preemptively alert him to our imminent return. He didn't respond, I began to suspect he was either busy or simply didn't receive the message. After all, the pod had been baking in the Martian sun for months, perhaps some of the solar-resistant coating was somehow stripped in a sandstorm and our electronics were slightly damaged.

I stood staring out of the porthole as we approached the docking bay. It was certainly a sight to behold after such… experiences. As a safety measure, I shut off the auto pilot system, engaged the manual override protocol, and manually guided the pod into the docking bay as precisely as I could, since I didn't trust any of our technology at this point.

After locking the craft's bow into the now-pressurized safety airlock, I threw the lever up to open the hatch. There was a slight pressure change, and my ears popped. Each of us entered the chamber and closed the pod hatch before opening the main station door and entering. There to greet us was Dr. Brogg, along with dozens of other former colleagues of mine which had assisted me with various other terraformation-related endeavors in the past. They had set up a welcome home party in anticipation of our return, complete with decorations, cake, music, a hearty meal, and gallons of soda. I wasn't even aware that the majority of these things were available aboard the MOSS.

"Welcome home, lads!

Congratulations on your safe return!" Dr. Brogg shouted. "How-" I began, but Dr. Brogg cut me off. "We've had the majority of this whole ordeal set up outside of the bay for the past few months, patiently awaiting your arrival. As soon as I received your transmission, I called for each research team and task force member to gather in front of Docking Bay A to surprise you. I figured you deserved a hero's welcome after enduring several months in a miserable cave!" "How did you know we were even alive and able to return?" I asked. "Oh, when you preside over manned missions as long as I have, it becomes gut instinct. I cant tell you how, John, I just knew. Come, sit at the head seat of the table, we'll munch on some dinner while you tell us what you've experienced, lad." I was shocked by Dr. Brogg's homecoming party, I

figured perhaps Brogg had
noticed a change in my demeanor
prior to our departure, or that he
somehow knew I'd been having
intrusive dreams, but there was no
way to tell what had prompted this
display of kindness. I did know,
however, that they weren't
expecting a story anywhere near
the magnitude of the one I'd just
experienced. Once everyone was
seated, Dr. Brogg spoke. "Aye,
lads! I'd like to propose a
toast," He raised his glass before
lowering it to his waist. "to the
bravest and most adventurous
interplanetary explorers we've
ever laid eyes upon. These men
have braved the Martian wilderness
in pursuit of humanity's destiny;
to inherit the stars and spread
life across the galaxy. God has
been gracious to us, and we ought
to give Him thanks for allowing
the safe return of these fine
young men." "Hear hear!" Everyone

shouted, as they clinked their glasses together and threw back their carbonated drinks. Nehemiah then stood to his feet. "If I may, I would like to lead us in prayer before I begin to devour my meal like a ravenous dog, because Lord knows I'm starving for decent food after choking down those beef brisket MREs." This comment was met with a few chuckles from around the table. "If you would, please stand." I stood to my feet, as did everyone else, and we bowed our heads in prayer, we all thanked God for the incredible things He'd done in our lives.

Once the prayer was concluded and we sank back into our chairs, I made an effort to contain my unease as I steeled myself for the reactions I would receive for my retelling of recent events. At the behest of Dr. Brogg, I began with our descent into the Martian atmosphere. As I delved deeper

into the story, I watched as
Brogg's face dropped, and my men
were visibly on edge, despite
having heard this same story once
before. When I attempted to
explain to them how the entity,
which I later discovered to be the
evil one, was visibly composed of
non-space, everyone's face in the
room betrayed a sense of primalp
terror. I continued my
recollection straight to that
moment, and Dr. Brogg was
dumbfounded. "So you've visited
multiple habitable planets,
including Jupiter and an unknown
moon?" He inquired. "I only know
what I've told you. I'm not so
sure I was there physically,
perhaps it was a spiritual vision
in which I was physically present.
Maybe they were physical locations
within the spiritual realm, or
perhaps I truly did visit other
stars. I'm not even certain to
what extent these apparent
'visions'

were fabricated to push a satanic narrative, but I can assure you that the concept of alien life is simply a work of fiction straight from the lying tongue of satan himself. These experiences have all but confirmed this, and I'm not entirely certain that we're meant to gather anything else from these events. There are some things mankind is simply not meant to have any knowledge of, in spite of our incessantly curious nature and relentless pursuit of knowledge. It is not biological and sentient alien life that we will war with, but we currently war with demonic forces which seek to undermine our faith in Christ and salvation, and to return our nation and our people to the liberal, materialistic, pagan, gender-confused child sacrifice cult that our fathers gave their lives to rescue us from. As it says in

Ephesians 6:12; 'For we do not wrestle against flesh and blood, but against the rulers, against the authorities, against the cosmic powers over this present darkness, against the spiritual forces of evil in the heavenly places.' We are to remain steadfast in the faith as our ancestors did, and run the race to the end as Paul describes in 1 Corinthians 9:24-27." "Hear, hear!" Everyone shouted in unison as they raised their glasses and clinked them together once more. As everyone's mood shifted to one of celebration following my concluding speech, Dr. Brogg seemed to sink into a despair, which he was trying in vain to hide. "Could you excuse me for a moment?" I said amidst the multiple conversations occurring around the table to no one in particular as I stood up and tapped Brogg on the shoulder,

hoping he'd understand that I
wished for him to follow me into
the next room.

"You look like you're having a
rough time, sir. What's the
issue?" I inquired. "I can't stop
pondering the implications of
this. Does this mean we should
continue colonizing the Solar
System as we are, or should we
cease doing so if there's no alien
life? If God is in control, and
there is no fear of our star dying
and destroying all life on Earth,
what is propelling us into the
realm of space travel to begin
with?" He asked. "Human nature.
Don't you see it, Dr. Brogg? With
God affirming that He is with us,
we have all the more reason to
advance technologically! We should
colonize the universe if God is
willing! Think of it like this,
sir. If God will it, it will be
done. Simply live life in
obedience to Him, and everything

will fall into place, you'll
see." "Matthew 6:33." He added.
"'*But seek ye first the Kingdom of
God and His righteousness, and all
these things shall be added unto
you.*'" I said, hoping to put his
mind at ease. We returned to the
table, and I finished my feast fit
for a king.

For the past two months, I've
been recording this log entry. I
began immediately following the
dinner, wanting to record what had
occurred while it was fresh in my
mind. It's now January 4th, 2101.

CHAPTER 11

PREPARATIONS

"Thus out of small beginnings greater things have been produced by His hand that made all things of nothing, and gives being to all things that are; and, as one small candle may light a thousand, so the light here kindled hath shone unto many, yea in some sort to our whole nation." -William Bradford

Entry 11: 01/21/2101
Dr. Brogg has decided that our research and preparation is sufficient enough to begin preparing for a full fledged colonial settlement on the surface of Mars. While we're all excited and the news back on Earth is repeatedly broadcasting several-hour-long talks on Martian Colonization, I think it would be best to avoid getting ahead of

ourselves. Dr. Brogg asked that I request several shipments of supplies and building materials from NASA to be delivered via unmanned pods, but the pods' arrival will take several weeks, not to mention the supply acquisitions and preparations NASA has to undergo on their end. Brogg is planning to send a significant portion of the men aboard the MOSS to set up sustainable greenhouses, water filtration systems, mining rigs, and a small village of radiation-proof solar huts. They're to be fully furnished as comfortably as the average American's home, and the dozens of shipments of supplies required to achieve this incredible feat will not arrive for a good while. In the meantime, I've briefed my team on a proposal I'd like to make to Dr. Brogg involving modifying the now-dormant oxygen converters to produce O3 (Ozone Gas) to create a protective barrier in the Martian stratosphere. The air is already relatively breathable; the surface, and even MOSS Cavern is likely heavily contaminated with microorganisms that hitchhiked on our persons, and the temperatures have increased just enough for a portion of the subsurface ice to melt and begin forming light clouds in certain areas of the planet, but no storms have been recorded thus far. My intention is to artificially generate a gaseous barrier which would prevent the sun's ultraviolet radiation from bombarding any life on the planet, and the biological activity from the flora and fauna I've ordered would produce enough "greenhouse emissions" to warm the atmosphere, thus fully terraforming Mars into a second Earth. I've requested 12 of every basic seed-bearing plant readily available to NASA. I plan to plant dozens of trees, crops,

and grass plants in an attempt
to kickstart the artificially
created ecosystem. If we're
careful enough, we'll be able to
create the ideal Earth, free of
any diseases, pests, or parasites.
A perfect unity between nature and
man, a utopia of Earthly life
existing in harmony, save for
cases of natural predation.

This may not be possible for a
number of reasons, including human
nature; man's inherent propensity
for pride, greed, violence, and
other abhorrent evils, but we
might as well use this opportunity
to definitively determine whether
or not the creation of such an
ecosystem is sustainable, or even
remotely feasible.

Entry 12: 02/12/2101

It's been days since my last entry. We've been enjoying some much needed R&R while awaiting the arrival of the materials we requisitioned for the establishment of our new colony. Now that I've caught up on some much needed rest and the mountain of paperwork that has been laying on my desk for the past few months, I've decided to create another log entry.

Just shy of two hours ago, after a brief conference in which my men and I proposed our plan to artificially generate an ozone layer on Mars, Dr. Brogg obliged, stating that he wants this project to be completed at least two weeks prior to the arrival of our supplies, for which NASA gave an estimated arrival date of 04/16/2101. I have once again assembled my team consisting of Henry, Jeremy, Nehemiah, and

Michael. I've ordered them each to take the next two days to prepare for a minimum of two weeks on the surface of Mars, warning them to pack any and all supplies they feel will be necessary. We have a general ground mission SOP binder on hand that contains a few packing list examples for such an occasion. I have fully clarified my intended results and expect to drop from orbit in two days. I will really only require provisions of food and water, as well as a basic toolbox to make the rather simplistic tweaks needed for the transmuters to function as intended.

Entry 13: 02/14/2101

There have been many suggestions floating around as to what we should name the new colony, considering it will likely become a city one day. I suppose it will soon be a requirement to specify your planet on your mailing address, though the logistics of interplanetary mailing seem far too complicated with our current technology. My men are ready, with their gear lying before Docking Bay A. We plan to touch down slightly past the Martian sunrise on the section of the planet housing the transmuters.

It's been a few hours since I last updated this entry. Our landing was smooth; we dropped our gear and began tweaking the transmuters, successfully converting and activating 23 of them so far. After running the numbers, I concluded that if we convert 75 transmuters in total, it will take no longer than two weeks to successfully convert 0.00006% of the Martian atmosphere to ozone, which should naturally form a concentrated protective layer approximately 17 miles above the surface of the planet. I've decided that our return date will be officially set for 02/22/2101, giving us time to manually disable the transmuters after they've served their intended purpose.

Entry 14: 02/23/2101

Today, we have officially returned from our mission, which was a complete success! The UV Radiations levels on the surface of the red planet have been reduced significantly, and much more of the subsurface ice sheets have melted into liquid rivers and streams. Lakes and streams of water which have remained dormant for thousands of years have begun flowing throughout the many crevasses and valleys present on Mars. Really, the final step in the terraformation process, aside from perhaps adjusting the artificial magnetic field generator slightly and installing a backup generator, is to import living organisms to incorporate into the planet's currently nonexistent ecosystem. We're still awaiting the arrival of the unmanned ships carrying our supplies, along with a few brave

colonists that volunteered to be
some of the first men to truly
live on Mars, though Dr. Brogg
mentioned that they could arrive
slightly earlier or later than
expected, depending on a number of
factors such as solar wind flare-
ups that cannot necessarily be
preemptively calculated. For now,
I believe we should focus on
preparing for the day everything
arrives, which would presumably be
April 16th, so we're ready to
begin the setup process
immediately after each ship docks.

Entry 15: 04/12/2101

As it turns out, the bulk of the
supply ships are due to dock
within the next twelve hours,
which would put them about three
days ahead of their expected
arrival time, which is splendid
news. I've been pondering the
political aspect of this soon-to-
be colony, and have been delving
into many early colonial American
works. I've read many books
recently written by our
forefathers which are teeming with
timeless wisdom. When our
ancestors landed in Plymouth over
480 years ago, they immediately
composed, signed, and thereby
established the Mayflower Compact
on November 11th, 1620; prior to
even stepping off their ship.
Their main objective in doing this
was to come to an agreement as to
how their colony was to be
governed before it's official
establishment, which has been

regarded by historians ever since as an incredible display of the wisdom of the men who founded our great nation. Their main points, which were outlined in the document, stated plainly that they were Christian men who were loyal to the King of England, would create fair and just legislation, and would work together for the good of Plymouth Colony. Though our ancestors were but a speck on a massive, untamed continent full of the most arduous terrain and living conditions on Earth, they remained steadfast in their efforts to settle the land and build the global empire that the rest of the world has benefitted from in tremendous ways for nearly 325 years. I believe that formulating a basis upon which this colony's legislative and political processes will function, formally agreed upon by all colonists, will benefit future

Martian societies in inconceivable ways. Drafting a document sufficiently outlining the style and form of government which we desire to establish will perhaps be the most important part of Martian history. Because of this, I plan to speak with Dr. Brogg one on one in his office later this evening to propose that we formally request that all imminently arriving colonists gather on the main floor of the MOSS soon after docking to coordinate in drafting such a document, making revisions and additions as we prepare the supplies and materials to descend to the surface. Because all Earthen societies have ardently banned all forms of usury and unnecessarily high taxation, which has been punishable by hanging for any political or government official found to be engaging in such acts since the 2nd

Revolution, we have no reason to
suspect that any (eventual)
Martian colony would spontaneously
yearn for rebellion. Presumably,
America will not tax the colonies
in any way. However, I would like
to leave every aspect of
governance to the colonies own
discretion beginning with my
proposed foundational charter,
giving them a certain level of
autonomy; but it is ultimately up
to the near-absolute authority the
US Government has given to Dr.
Brogg concerning Martian colonial
affairs.

CHAPTER 12

MOSS COLONY

"Among the natural rights of the colonists are these: First a right to life, secondly to liberty, and thirdly to property; together with the right to defend them in the best manner they can. These are evident branches of... the duty of self-preservation, commonly called the first law of nature. All men have a right to remain in a state of nature as long as they please; and in the case of intolerable oppression, civil or religious, to leave the society they belong to, and enter into another... Now what liberty can there be where property is taken away without consent?"

-Samuel Adams

Entry 16: 05/03/2101

The goods finally arrived within two hours of completing my last entry on April 12th, a full ten hours shy of the final ETA. I'd already spoken to Dr. Brogg an hour prior regarding my "Mayflower Compact" proposal, and he agreed that it would help ease any eventual confusion in the organization of Martian colonial governments. Once the men and supplies had arrived, we greeted them at the docking bays. After pulling the bulk of their supplies from their pods and reorganizing everything in preparation for setuo, I explained to them our desire to establish an agreed-upon founding document to aid in the creation of any future government. and they happily obliged, drafting a lengthy, single-page document over several hours, discussing ardently the contents therein. The full document reads as follows:

171

We the PEOPLE of MOSS COLONY seek to establish order within our settlement as to dispel confusion and political strife. First, all men of MOSS must be able to worship God in peace above all; second, it is imperative to ensure that NO man be deprived of arms of ANY SORT, which are the cornerstone of free societies, as tyrannical, authoritarian regimes will always arise in their absence; third, NO man may be deprived of his right to speak FREELY and OPENLY that which he believes to be true OR OTHERWISE, that which is considered free speech MAY NOT be dictated by government NOR private entities in any fashion, any dictation or restriction of speech shall therefore warrant a revolution to restore these freedoms which were bestowed upon mankind by GOD, and which the United States of America seeks to perpetually recognize.; fourth, no man may own or operate any business entity which can be proven harms the general populace on an evidentiary basis. Such an entity is subject to being dismantled entirely at the behest of WE THE PEOPLE on charges of immoral activities; fifth, no governing body may impose any tax on income whatsoever, as this is a hinderance to the wealth and prosperity of the working class, whom the remainder of society owes a debt of gratitude toward; sixth, no government, public, or

*private entity whatsoever may seize any property
lawfully obtained by any citizen or other entity; finally,
the colonies shall have the right to secede and govern
themselves autonomously in any manner they deem fit,
pursuant to the terms outlined in this founding document.*

Notice we added a clause to ensure the rights of any Martian colonies to secede from the union. This is in honor of, and taken from the wisdom gained from both revolutionary wars. The first was waged against Britain, King George III in particular, over unfair taxation, and the government of our ancestral land micromanaging our colonies. From our victory forward, we recognized the right of the people to keep and bear arms, ensuring their right to overthrow any future tyrannical governments. The second revolution was waged against the most oppressive, violent, and evil

regime in human history over
many issues which the ballot box
seemed unable to resolve. After
our victory, our fathers
reinforced the US Constitution to
dispel all doubt surrounding each
amendment, and to codify basic
Christian principles into law.
There is no longer any question of
whether a corporation has a right
to censor or outright ban any man
from speaking or publicizing his
opinion. There can be no
administrative nor legal
punishment from any public or
private institutions whatsoever
for expressing any beliefs or
opinions. As our ancestors knew,
yet failed to fully outline in
proper detail, (though one would
would assume it to be unnecessary,
2ARW History has proven it
necessary) these principles are
foundational to any society's
long-term success, so we codified
them into MOSS Colony's laws.

Once we were all satisfied that this represented our desires for governmental parameters, each of the men present signed the document, with Dr Brogg's signature being the most prominent as the authority representing the United States.

After reorganizing all that we needed to set up MOSS Colony, we ordered each of the men to enter pods. I had already ordered Henry, Michael, Jeremy, and Nehemiah to enter our same pod in Docking Bay A. We activated auto drop, input the longitude and latitude of where we had agreed to set up the colony, and smacked the drop button.

During our descent, one of the pods carrying supplies suffered a major hardware failure, and the auto pilot system disengaged and the entire system shut down, somehow circumventing the need for prior authorization, which was thought to be next to impossible. Thinking on my feet, I activated five of our rovers which were still docked onboard our pod, and commanded them using my geolometer's interface to slide under the falling pod and use their thrusters to ensure it landed safely. We touched down on the red planet, exited our pods, and began extricating supplies from the storage compartments. I grabbed my clipboard, which listed everything we were to have brought with us, and ordered everyone to lay out their supplies and gear for an inspection to ensure everything had arrived safely. Once everyone had confirmed that they had accounted for their gear, supplies, and building materials, I made my rounds, marking off everything I saw to double check. Sure enough, everything was there. All of the colonists were skilled in construction, as well as a

number of other fields, so when
I handed them each building's
corresponding charts, blueprints,
and notes, they began building
them straight away.

As they assembled their
dwellings, I pulled the
assortments of various seeds and
plants from one of the pods and
began surveying the area for good
places to plant certain trees and
grass. I had a specific set of
seeds and full-grown plants set
aside for the colonial greenhouse,
but still took one of each seed/
plant to attempt to kickstart
their wild Martian population.
Though there were no plant
populations on Mars at the moment,
I still brought along several
species of both male and female
freshwater fish, including
bluegill, bass, crappie, catfish,
trout, walleye, salmon, pike,
minnow, shad, and bowfin, among
others; as well as thousands of

juvenile crayfish, thirty-two
hundred hundred gallons of
tightly-packed mixed algae and
freshwater plant life,
zooplankton, and various aquatic
insects. I figured this would be
enough to begin introducing a
fully sustainable ecosystem into
the many freshwater lakes and
rivers which were so abundant on
Mars. I also brought along cattail
(bulrush/reedmace) seeds, lily pad
seeds, among many other freshwater
shore-dwelling plants. I enlisted
the help of Michael and Henry to
space out many of the seeds I was
planting, being mindful of the
conditions which may affect each
species. I used my geolometer to
determine which plants would be
best suited to live in certain
climates on the planet. Realizing
that I needed to travel the planet
to truly jumpstart the Martian
ecosystem, I began searching for a
vehicle of some sort. We were able

to convert three rovers into a vehicle capable of traversing the Martian surface at around 250mph.

After several hours of planting and dumping algae-water and fish into streams, I began targeting the more massive lakes, working my way down to the more pond-sized bodies of water. We had brought along many year-old trees in pots, which we chose specific locations to plant based on what climate they were best suited for. Many of the larger lakes were now teeming with fish, algae, turtles, and cattails. Though there were a few smaller interconnected oceans scattered across Mars, it seemed any eventual ocean life would have to await the next shipment. After gazing upon the work we'd done, I grew confident that any life we brought to the planet would survive and thrive.

Entry 17: 07/09/2101

We've been hard at work making
the new colonists feel at home
while they begin settling the
land. A few have already begun
successfully growing acres of
various species of grass in their
yards. Many of the trees visible
from the colony have dropped
seeds, and will hopefully
propagate into forests if all goes
well. The greenhouse is overtaken
by fruit-bearing plants of all
sorts. I sent a small fleet of our
rovers to the East to begin
digging a mine where strong
signatures of gold, nickel, and
iron were detected. There should
be enough in that general area to
supply a small city. I've decided
to order 1,000 of each known tree
species which is gauged to have
reasonable survivability odds for
shipment to the MOSS, as I believe
this will quickly generate the
ideal environment to introduce

several animal species. I an
thoroughly convinced that Mars is
able to become a utopian society
free of many of the ecological
issues plaguing Earthly life. Only
time will truly tell, however. For
now, it seems the colony will run
smoothly on it's own, continuing
to grow and settle the world
without need for my intervention.
I've decided that my men and I
will return to the MOSS tomorrow
morning.

CHAPTER 13

SCOUTING MISSION

"I can calculate the movement of stars, but not the madness of men." -Isaac Newton

Entry 18: 07/21/2101
We finally returned to the MOSS on the 13th. The colony has continued to run smoothly and is actively assisting the wildlife in flourishing and populating the planet. For now, we have other matters to tend to. Dr. Brogg has been sending multiple transmissions to Earth, discussing the possibility of scouting other celestial bodies in our Solar System which may be suitable for colonization. Following the incredible potential that Mars is showing, NASA authorities are quite seriously considering scouting for another planet to

terraform, and to repeat this
same process using the immense
knowledge we've gathered over the
course of our research on the
MOSS, which will surely streamline
the process for any future
colonization endeavors. Brogg is
wanting to use an unmanned drone
equipped with a fleet of 10 rovers
to explore Venus, and Jupiter's
moons Europa, IO, and Ganymede, as
well as the "dwarf" planet Pluto
to rule them out as candidates for
colonization. In my speculation,
I'd assume that colonizing Pluto
would likely require the careful
research of an orbital space
station similar to the MOSS. I do
believe that, in terms of oceanic
terraformation, Europa is
certainly a reasonable candidate,
considering that moon houses an
ocean buried under an ice sheet
containing more water than all of
Earth's bodies of water combined.
As for IO and Ganymede, I would

presume that their settlement is ultimately a pipe dream, for now. Dr. Brogg has formally invited my team and I to operate the craft and fleet of rovers on each assigned exploratory mission from a makeshift control room on the MOSS. He's made it clear however, that if it should be discovered that Europa or Venus are viable, we are to return to Earth before boarding a craft to embark on a manned exploratory mission, something I'm not looking forward to should that need arise.

Entry 19: 08/23/2101

We sent two rovers on a scouting
mission on July 21st. One was sent
to Venus, the other to the surface
of Europa. On the 23rd of July, we
sent out two more rovers; one to
the surface of IO, and one to
Ganymede. Both of our initial
scout rovers made a safe landing
mere hours ago, with our other two
only hours away from their
destination.
Thanks to rather recent
advancements in quantum computing,
I've acquired a remote comms
system capable of signaling the
rovers nearly instantaneously,
despite the incredible distance.
We've also begun utilizing this
technology to rapidly communicate
with NASA. Before I stepped out
from the control room to eat my
lunch and type out a new log entry
while leaving Henry in charge, I
was remotely operating the Europa
rover's digital

interface and actively exploring
the Jovian moon. From the rover's
vast arsenal of automated tools, I
deployed a drill to clear a
sloped, traversable path into the
depths of the thick ice layer that
blankets the world. Turning my
attention to Venus, I ran numerous
tests to ascertain the true
atmospheric composition and to
discover if there was any trace of
a natural magnetosphere. I was
aware of the atmosphere of Venus
producing what is known as an
induced magnetosphere, which is
generated by solar winds carrying
the sun's magnetic field, which
then interacts with the ionosphere
of Venus to generate an induced
magnetic field which protects the
planet's unusually thick
atmosphere as solar winds blow
past it. However, we will likely
need a stronger magnetosphere to
successfully terraform such a
hostile and uninhabitable planet.

The atmosphere on Venus is roughly composed of 96%-97% Carbon Dioxide and 3%-5% Nitrogen, among trace amounts of other gases, though I have the exact empirical data we've recorded on a chart in the control room. I've decided to consult with Dr. Brogg regarding the possibility of placing CO_2-O_2 transmuters on the surface of Venus and attempting to preemptively skew the atmospheric composition to be more Earth-like. I've also set the Venus rover to auto-pilot, with the sole directive of analyzing soil composition and exploring any cave systems it discovers to ascertain what resources are most abundant, as well as the planet's approximate water composition. I'll update this log once we've drilled into the ice sheets of Europa.

Entry 20: 09/13/2101

Oddly enough, the CO_2 transmuters have already arrived on the surface of Venus. After collecting the data gathered from the various soil and mineral analyses conducted by our rover, I redirected it's attention to automatically setting the transmuters up. The ice sheets of Europa are much thinner than we'd previously believed. We were streaming our video feed from the rover back to NASA, who shared it with the world on live television. The world watched in awe and wonder as the rover's drill finally hit liquid water after a stunning 25 miles of following an oblique path. Once the man-sized tunnel was fully constructed, we converted the rover into an aquatic unmanned vehicle and scoured the oceans in search of… well, whatever we could discover. No one really had a preconceived

notion of what we might find
under the ice except rocks and
crystal clear waters. We had
estimated that the oceans under
the ice sheets of Europa could
extend up to 100 miles deep, but
we wouldn't know for certain until
today. The world watched in wonder
and amazement at God's incredible
work as we continued our
exploration. All we'd seen up to
this point was a seemingly
bottomless body of water below the
rover, and the ice sheet floating
above. As the rover traversed
vertically along the bottom of the
ice sheet, a rock formation
appeared in the distance,
approximately 200 feet below the
rover. I immediately signaled the
rover to dive toward it, hoping it
was connected to a sea bed and not
simply suspended a few thousand
feet above the ocean floor. Once
the rover had approached the rock
formation, it was apparent that it

was somehow connected to the sea floor, though the spike-shaped rock was possibly several thousand feet tall, as although the sunlight penetrated the ice sheets unexpectedly well, it was too dim to see anything beyond 500 feet below sea level without the specialized lighting equipment that the rover carried. After the rover had descended following the protruding rock a whopping 58,000 feet, it finally reached the bottom… of the rock. The ocean floor was still nowhere in sight, despite a nearly 11 mile descent. The mere thought of Earth's oceans being anywhere near as deep as Europa's paralyzes me with terror at what sort of creatures could have dwelt in such an environment.

I signaled the rover to descend so we could begin exploring the deepest pits of the moon's oceans. I've set the rover to auto pilot as it scans and generates a map of the ocean floor, which should be complete in a few months. In the meantime, we'll be monitoring the progress of the transmuters on Venus in anticipation of increasing it's habitability enough to convince Earthside authorities to form an organization dedicated to Venus colonization, similar to our's.

Entry 21: 12/25/2101

Once the transmuters had successfully balanced the atmosphere of Venus, I proposed to Dr. Brogg that we run the idea by NASA to form a Venus Colonization task force, and that we share the many breakthroughs we've made with them. He agreed, but admitted that he'd already attempted to do the same with Europa, but they stipulated that the entire ocean must be mapped and all anomalies or potential hazards and hinderances be catalogued before they'd volunteer any resources for formulating such an organization. Considering Venus has been studied and mapped for as many decades as Mars has, it shouldn't be nearly as much of an issue. Once I'd exited my consultation with Dr. Brogg, I immediately ordered each of my men; Michael, Henry, Jeremy, and Nehemiah to work 24/7 on ensuring that rover maps every square inch of Europa. I organized their shift schedule so that each one would work a twelve hour shift every two days, starting with Michael. I figured it would give them plenty of down time to rest and relax.

I decided to dedicate myself to helping Dr. Brogg with building a convincing case for the formation of a Venus Colonization task force, starting by analyzing a three dimensional topographical map which displayed cave systems already mapped by previous exploratory missions NASA had conducted many years ago. We concluded that there were only two cave systems, neither of which would require any additional exploration to aid in mapping. As for seismic and volcanic activity, though volcanically active, there haven't been any known major volcanic eruptions on the planet since 2079, and NASA has been keeping tabs on which areas of Venus would pose the most risk to any colonists. Seismic activity is of no concern and seemingly poses no risk whatsoever. The only issue we have to face, and an admittedly major one, is the surface temperature. It usually hits a whopping 860°F (464°C) or higher due to it being in close proximity to the sun, and it's atmosphere being thick enough to trap heat at a significant rate. We have many methods of mitigating this, but the most promising seems to be to build an artificial "solar shield" capable of withstanding almost any damage, while generating energy and cooling the planet even slightly below Earth's average temperature at it's equator. Dr. Brogg has already requested that such a contraption be built and shipped directly to Venus for our rover to remotely construct, obviously adding that it must be

constructed with a coating of
our new indestructible alloy.

  This may be more of a personal
or philosophical musing, but I'm
very grateful that my voice is
heard in this post-revolution,
anti-corporatism, and anti-liberal
society. It seems we're
progressing at an extraordinary
rate as we begin to colonize the
galaxy one planet at a time. I've
heard from a colleague of mine
here on the MOSS that an
independent organization
specializing in space tech is
developing a manned spacecraft
which could travel 80,000,000Mph,
which is around 100x faster than
our fastest known manned
spacecraft. They also claim to
have build a device capable of
harnessing energy from a fusion
reactor, or a small man-made star,
but the technology to create and
sustain such a reaction, as well
as the immense heat generated from

it, is still far out of reach
for the time being. If this
concept is ever furthered, we may
gain the ability to travel near,
at, or potentially even faster
than the speed of light, though
it's heavily debated as to whether
faster-than-light travel is
possible based on our
understanding of the laws of
physics. As exciting as this is, I
don't think my generation will be
the one to create such an
incredible engineering feat.

If I want to improve my
(eventual) descendants' lives, I
need to work with what I have,
which seems to be pioneering the
terraformation of the solar
system.

CHAPTER 14

THE ASSISTANT DIRECTOR

"Yes, we are the nation of progress, of individual freedom, of universal enfranchisement. Equality of rights is the cynosure of our union of States, the grand exemplar of the correlative equality of individuals; and while truth sheds its effulgence, we cannot retrograde, without dissolving the one and subverting the other. We must onward to the fulfillment of our mission — to the entire development of the principle of our organization — freedom of conscience, freedom of person, freedom of trade and business pursuits, universality of freedom and equality. This is our high destiny, and in nature's eternal, inevitable decree of cause and effect we must accomplish it. All this will be our future history, to establish on earth the moral dignity and salvation of man — the immutable truth and beneficence of God. For this blessed mission to the nations of the world, which are shut out from the life-giving light of truth, has America been chosen; and her high example shall smite unto death the tyranny of kings, hierarchs, and oligarchs, and carry the glad tidings of peace and good will where myriads now endure an existence scarcely more enviable than that of beasts of the field. Who, then, can doubt that our country is destined to be the great nation of futurity? -John O'Sullivan, 1839

Entry 22: 02/13/2102

NASA scrambled to invent a planet wide solar shield for Venus, swiftly sending it to the rover aboard an unmanned craft, which arrived not long ago. Considering the haste with which they'd assembled this untested device, we ran a few remote function tests of our own via the rover to ascertain it's durability and longevity, and were pleased with our results. The strange contraption has been functional for around three weeks now, and the average recorded surface temperature has dropped from 860°F to an incredible 215°F (101.6°C),

and our researchers predict a
continuance of this steady decline
until the temperatures reach an
average of 75°F (23.8°C). As for
Europa, we've mapped the entirety
of the surface in 4K resolution
images which have been stitched
together. Europa can now be
viewed via a three-dimensional
image of the moon which can be
magnified to reveal near-
microscopic details on every inch
of the surface. The ocean floor is
also 87% mapped as of now, there
is minimal volcanic activity on
the seabed, and of course, no life
has been discovered anywhere.
We've continued scouring every
inch of the sea and have
discovered nothing of value.
Because of this, I met with Dr.
Brogg and discussed sending word
to NASA that their stipulations
have been met, and he agreed,
stating that he has full
confidence that there are no major

hazards on the satellite, but that we will continue to allow the rover to map the remainder of the ocean floor for our peace of mind. Once we'd sent word, NASA gathered in their meeting chambers to discuss what actions they were

taking regarding colonization in general, deliberating on many key elements in organizing future endeavors. Finally, we received word that they'd decided to move forward with allocating any resources we felt were necessary to further our colonizations efforts. They decided to dismantle the MOSS research group. This wasn't bad news, however, as they also decided to form a new department of the United States federal government which they named: "The United States Department Of Interstellar Colonization." They formally requested that Dr. Brogg agree to a promotion to director of this new department, and that I agree to my appointment to the role of assistant director, which we both graciously accepted. Ultimately, you could say that our operations were simply elevated to a federal level. From here, they decided to create divisions of this department for each planet we were colonizing, and implemented a clause into the massive framework of founding paperwork which ensured that each colony would be governed entirely independent of Earth once founded and self-sustaining. A part of our organization's job is also to ensure the longevity of the colonies and continue to assist them in any way necessary following their independence. Since each planet or moon would now have it's own division of the USDIC, Dr. Brogg left me in charge of appointing the head of each one. I decided to appoint Henry as the new head of the Martian Colonial Task Force Division, or MCD as it was abbreviated. I also appointed Michael as the head of the Venus Colonial Task Force Division (VCD), and Nehemiah as the Europa Colonial Task Force Division (ECD). I personally felt that it would only be fair to consult with the men of MOSS Colony as to whether they approved of this new initiative. Once I'd explained everything to them on a video call, I received resounding support for the new federal organization, which encouraged me to push harder for the colonization of both Venus and Europa.

As I ponder my encounters with the evil one, I can't help but consider that future historians, in an era of revived materialism and debauchery when the birthing pains of Revelation can be restrained no longer, may look upon my records with mockery and contempt, doubting that such a thing could ever have occurred. I pray for those future generations of men, that they may turn from their ways when the inevitable end arrives as prophesied by Christ. Though I wish I had more to add regarding what I'd experienced, I'm afraid I simply don't. The interpretation of what I've shared with the world will ultimately be left in the hands of future generations that seek to study the lives of the great men who began exploring the incredible frontier of space.

Earthside authorities at NASA have confirmed that they are stockpiling enough resources to colonize multiple planets, and that it is up to Dr. Brogg and I's discernment as to which planets and moons we target next, as with the many scientific hurdles we've overcome, it seems we now have the technology to colonize nearly any rocky celestial body. They've also sent word that they plan to send the families of the colonists on Mars once they've more firmly established the new planetary ecosystem and have kickstarted much of the infrastructure needed to begin an advanced civilization. They want the colonists to populate Mars rather than sending "interplanetary immigrants" to bolster the population. This same precedent will likely be adhered to in the colonization of future worlds. Because a physicist recently proved via a complex mathematical formula that faster-than-light travel is feasible, my recommendation is to fund faster-than-light travel research and push for the ability to travel to other stellar systems to explore and colonize their worlds. Of course, I believe the best way to do this would be to send orbital

space stations similar to the
MOSS, housing the potential
colonists, to each planet of each
star we're studying to determine
whether they're suitable for
colonization, as well as to
discover any variables that should
be taken into consideration. I've
brought this up to NASA
executives, but the technology
still seems to be far from
realized. For now, I think Venus
is suitable for the beginning
stages of colonization. As for
Europa, I think we can send pods
carrying marine life, but human
colonization is nearly impossible
due to the only habitable portion
of the satellite being entirely
submersed in an ocean.

Entry 23: 04/13/2102

Europa is now inhabited by a variety of marine life which seems to be thriving quite well in the depths of it's oceans. We may simply leave our rover on Europa to study and catalogue the various effects of the satellite's conditions on the aquatic life. The various flora and fauna we've brought to Mars has been incredibly successful in engulfing the planet in a sea of vegetation. For the time being, we've decided to focus merely on advancing the colonization of Venus, as well as assisting the Martian colonists in any matter we're able. We've given the colonists a direct line to NASA for requesting trivial supplies and building materials should any need of them arise. It seems they still haven't implemented any system of government, though such a thing could take decades, since self-

governance seems to be at the
bottom of their list of their
concerns. I've scheduled a
consultation with Dr. Brogg, as
well as Michael, our head of the
Venus Colonization Task Force
Division, to come to an agreement
as to how and when we should
proceed.

Entry 24: 09/13/2102

It took *much* longer than anticipated to fully stabilize the atmosphere of Venus for unsheltered colonization, but the planet's conditions are now ideal for a thriving ecosystem and colonial settlement. After consulting with Dr. Brogg and Michael regarding our next step, we've decided on a full list of supply requisitions for the initial settlement of Venus. We've requested several industrial grade tools, materials for basic buildings, farm equipment, and dozens of both seeds and live potted plants to begin cultivating vegetation on Venus. These are essentially the same supplies we requested for Martian colonization, though this time we've decided to allow the 25 hand-picked colonists to bring their families on their initial trip. We've specifically asked

NASA to send the pods carrying the men and supplies directly to Venus. Michael, Dr. Brogg, and I will all meet them on the planet's surface by taking a pod from one of the docking bays, which *should* have no issue with interplanetary travel if we carry spare fuel on board. We will enter the atmosphere at approximately 1700 Hours United States Eastern Standard Time on 9/18 in anticipation of their arrival, bringing along a few dozen herbs and grasses that Michael has propagated and grown in his spare time as a housewarming gift.

We've also ordered fourteen dozen pods filled with various fauna from Earth which environmental scientists on the MOSS have determined would be the most suitable for inhabiting the newly created Martian environment. There is a climate on Mars for nearly every animal on Earth, save for some which only survive in certain extreme conditions. The vegetation on Mars has spread globally, which provides the ideal environment for millions of species. The colonists have cultivated dozens of acres and have built a full-fledged society, even creating their own technology. Because of this incredible display of fortitude and competence, Dr. Brogg has decided to give MOSS Colony their complete independence earlier than stipulated in their charter. However, we will continue to support their efforts in any way we can.

Entry 25: 09/18/2102

Only a few hours ago, we landed
on the surface of Venus and
greeted our new colonial friends
and congratulated them on
embarking on this exciting quest
to spread God's gift of life
across the cosmos. Dr. Brogg and I
then decided it would be best to
type up an original charter
similar to the MOSS Charter/
Compact we'd previously created.
They decided on the name
"Vesuvius" for the colony, though
it wasn't exactly clear to me what
has influenced this decision, it
was entirely the choice of the
colonists. Once everything was
agreed upon, the basic principles
read similar, except for one
particular clause. "*WE THE
PEOPLE of Vesuvius wish to enshrine into our initial
charter that we shall never fail to provide material
assistance to any other human settlement, as what we
have done for the least of these, we have done for our
LORD. By the*

grace of our *LORD JESUS THE CHRIST the people of Vesuvius wish to aid in the good work the LORD is doing through the USDIC.*" Once the terms of the charter were agreed upon as written and all were satisfied that it represented their desired future direction of their settlement, we then set up some makeshift huts for the women and children of the men to temporarily reside in while we each began building permanent structures to jumpstart the settlement. I assigned Michael to a small group tasked with properly planting the vegetation we had brought to best allow it to thrive and eventually reproduce globally, which had occurred at an incredibly fast pace on Mars. It's been a few hours since we began, and we've already built around 80% of the colony's infrastructure. I'm resting and eating an MRE as I write this log. I'd better get back to it.

Entry 26: 10/27/2102

The colony is now thriving. Once
we were all satisfied that the
colony of Vesuvius was well
established and nearly autonomous,
we once again boarded our pod and
digitally charted a course for the
MOSS directly to Docking Bay A,
which the autopilot system would
follow. Once we've returned, I
plan to check in on Europa and
MOSS colony.

Entry 27: 11/06/2102

We've finally returned from our
interplanetary voyage. While we
were away, Henry has been
carefully monitoring the progress
of MOSS Colony, and they've
continued thriving and cultivating
an incredible planetary ecosystem.
They've continued advancing and
have built a rather sizable
civilization considering their
rather small population of 127, 23
of which are children which were
born on Martian soil. I had a chat
with Henry about the possibility
of assisting MOSS Colony with
becoming it's own sovereign nation
and setting up a preliminary
system of government. That seems
to be a new ongoing project of
his, but he'll have to get the
colonist's approval to move
forward considering they're fully
recognized as independent by the
United States. Nehemiah has also
been doing his due diligence in

monitoring the development of our artificially created oceanic ecosystem on Europa via the rover. The aquatic plant life has rapidly reproduced and spread to every corner of the moon, and it's created such an abundant food source for marine animals that their populations have all exploded. It seems we're doing something right.

CHAPTER 15

INTERSTELLAR ADVANCEMENTS

"Gravity explains the motions of the planets, but it cannot explain who set the planets in motion. God governs all things and knows all that is or can be done." -Isaac Newton

Entry 28: 10/04/2103
It's been nearly a year since my last entry. We've continued our operations as usual. MOSS Colony is now the MOSS States of Mars, which is quite a peculiar name in my opinion, but their governor, who is now the democratically elected president of their constitutional republic, has been granted authority by his constituents to name the colony and help plan their future infrastructure, as well as implement new legislation which he deems necessary. The nation will

now grow exponentially in the coming centuries just as America did in it's infancy. They've also convened and agreed to send a certain number of settlers to select areas of the planet and begin their own "colonies" which will eventually grow to become sovereign Martian nations, but their population will need to triple at minimum before that plan is viable. The planet is becoming more of a paradise with each passing week, it is currently devoid of disease, famine, parasites, weeds, and pests; an ideal environment for humanity to thrive.

The colony of Vesuvius is now officially independent as of last month, though they still have a long way to go. Nearly the entire planet is blanketed in greenery and teeming with animal life, likely due to the rather high concentrations of oxygen in the atmosphere. Oxygen toxicity was a major concern of USDIC scientists, but the current levels seem to be slightly more ideal for life than the oxygen levels found on Earth. Their population has also grown exponentially, but out of their 126 adult colonists and 71 children born in Earth, there have been 57 children born on Venus since the founding of Vesuvius, bringing their total population to a whooping 254 colonists. Their infrastructure is hardly matching their population growth, but they're managing nonetheless. The entire point of colonization is to be fruitful and spread life across the galaxy as I've mentioned in previous entries, so this is all according to plan.

Europa is now as populated with aquatic life as the oceans of Earth, the rapid reproduction and spread of life throughout the satellite's oceans has baffled many of my colleagues. They hadn't thought it possible for a small number of any given species to conquer a planet in such a short span. We will continue to monitor each colony and monitor their progress over the coming years.

Entry 29: 12/24/2103

NASA just announced today that the first fully-functional nuclear fusion reactor is stable and active, and lends enough energy to power the recently conceptualized faster-than-light engine I've mentioned in a previous entry. This has now enabled humanity to travel to a few of the nearest stars in approximately 2 years according to researchers, which means we can begin interplanetary colonization soon. It's difficult for me to fully grasp the sudden shift from the mainstream scientific narrative of *"Faster-than-light travel is, and will always be impossible according the the laws of physics!"* to *"We're going to travel faster than the speed of light within the next few months!"* NASA has already begun constructing four massive ships capable of carrying an orbital space station across the vast

expanse that lies between our
Sun and the four closest
neighboring stars. They've
selected one planet from each
star's orbit that they've
determined to be the most viable
candidates for colonization, and
plan to send an orbital research
station to each one. Our four
closest neighboring stars are:
Proxima Centauri (and Alpha
Centauri) of which Proxima b
orbits in the red dwarf's
habitable zone; Wolf 359 of which
Wolf 359c orbits outside of the
red dwarf star's habitable zone,
though the planet is relentlessly
bombarded by three times as much
radiation as Earth; Lalande of
which Lalande 21185 (also known as
BD+36 2147, Gliese 411, and HD
95735) orbits outside of the red
dwarf star's habitable zone, yet
may still be suitable for
terraformation; and Leyuten of
which Leyuten b (also referred to

as Gliese 273b) orbits within the red dwarf star's habitable zone. As you've likely already noted, each of these planets will pose incredible challenges in terraformation, which will allow us to advance our terraformation techniques and further develop the technology we need to ultimately colonize every galaxy in the universe. Mankind has been made in the image of God, who has bestowed upon him stewardship over all creation. Man will soon fulfill his destiny to inherit the stars. This is quite an exciting opportunity, and I'm not sure what more I could add that would fully convey the reactions the world has given to this news. Awe and wonder, as well as a deep desire to explore the unknown has once again been reawakened in the hearts of men. These are incredible times we live in. Soon, the new ships will be built, and their engines developed and installed, and it will likely be left to Dr. Brogg and I to determine what supplies each crew should take on their voyage into uncharted territory. I will update this log soon. For now, Merry Christmas to all who read this work.

Entry 30: 03/16/2104

All four ships have been built and outfitted with engines capable of harnessing the immense power produced within a nuclear fusion reaction. According to NASA scientists, these engines are more than capable of traveling at 2.5x the speed of light once they've left Earth's atmosphere and have been oriented toward their destination. The only remaining step in this incredible and unprecedented leap into interstellar travel is to tweak the technology until it's foolproof, which will only take another month or two. Authorities at NASA are already contemplating who they'd select for such a mission, considering many renowned terraformation specialists from a pool of worthy candidates. As far as I'm aware, they haven't made any mention of who they'd like to head the operation, but

considering we're the United
States Department Of Interstellar
Colonization, I'd venture to guess
they'll tack this project onto our
duties once the ships have
embarked on their maiden voyage to
their respective stars. In the
meantime, MOSS and Vesuvius have
been steadily growing and
advancing. For the time being,
colonizing Europa with human life
is still off the table. It's not
technologically feasible for what
little benefit it would provide.
The majority of humanity is
eagerly anticipating our
advancement toward interstellar
travel, dreaming of America's
newest and final frontier; the
stars.

Entry 32: 05/21/2104

NASA finally launched the ships! The craft were named A2Proxima b, WolfA1359c, LalandeA321185, and LeyutenA4 b, each after their target planet. After carefully testing and tweaking every aspect of the crafts' engines and the fusion reactors themselves, as well as selecting four massive teams of scientists and gathering their families, they're finally off! This is a day in history more monumental than the famed moon landing. Accounts of this day will be echoed across the universe for all time! NASA has placed Dr. Brogg over the operation and has tasked him and I with ensuring the initial terraformation is a success. It will, however, take at least 2 years for most of the ships hauling the orbital research stations to reach their destinations, which gives us time to preemptively strategize as much

as possible on our end. There's
not much to ponder or take into
consideration in terms of what
equipment they'll use or what
plant or animal life they'll
colonize their planet with since
their ships have been outfitted
with every tool and resource they
could conceivably require, though
we would be able to send them
spare supplies should they need
any. Their water, oxygen, and food
supplies are designed to be mostly
self-sustaining, with minimal
human intervention required to
upkeep the cycles. Their water is
seamlessly recycled through
incredibly complex reverse-osmosis
filtration systems, their oxygen
is replenished via massive tanks
of algae that generate much more
oxygen per day than the humans and
animals residing on the ships
require, and they have a 150 year
supply of food on board, along
with a hydroponic garden which

yields enough vegetables to sustain them regardless. Their electricity, of course, is harvested from the sun via solar panels, as well as a few small solar-wind propelled windmills which could generate enough electricity to power a small city when spinning at maximum speed. NASA felt that this "over-preparation" was necessary to ensure the long-term survivability of the colonists should anything go awry in the terraformation processes of any of the planets.

With all of these considerations made for us, the only issue I can reasonably foresee is an issue with their technical equipment, such as their newly-updated atmospheric transmuters which can be set to convert whichever gas you desire into another. If one of those machines were to suffer a major technical malfunction, it would be difficult, or perhaps impossible for them to repair the issue on their own without a new shipment of parts. There's not much we can do to mediate this risk, though I've spoken with Dr. Brogg regarding the possibility of preparing a fleet of supply ships ahead of time so we're always prepared to respond to any issues they face. It could simply be because humanity has never ventured beyond the Sun, but we're all on edge. We've held many services in the chapel on the MOSS recently and have prayed that the men and their families be granted by God safe passage across the vast expanse of the cosmos which they're traversing. I suppose at a certain point, you have to leave your fate entirely in the hands of God Almighty. Not that it isn't always in His hands to begin with.

Entry 33: 06/29/2104

It's been only a month or so since the ships departed. We've received a total of two transmissions from each ship, simple messages letting us know that they've remained safe and on course. MOSS Colony already began choosing locations to build new nation-states once the young native martians of their number age. Vesuvius has decided to expand their colony and begin scouting new locations as well. There hasn't been any need of my intervention in their respective department's affairs for some time, and with their full independence officially declared, there's not much I could do for them without impeding their autonomy regardless. They are both a noble and cohesive people who will surely build two of the most incredible societies in the Milky Way.

Entry 34: 09/17/2107

This may be my last log entry. I haven't recorded anything for roughly three years now considering nothing really notable has occurred until today. Our each of the ships have now arrived at their destinations and are each orbiting their respective planet. Unbeknownst to me until the past few hours, NASA has assigned a select duo from each potential colony the task of studying the planet's host star in hopes of better understanding the various types of nuclear fusion reactions, and not only creating an infinite energy source, but invincible, eternal stars which can never be extinguished by natural means such as deteriorating into supernovae, though these men who specialize in solar sciences freely admit that it may very well take several thousand years to develop such technology, but this is as good a starting point as any.

MOSS and Vesuvius are now nearly indistinguishable from Earthen societies. Their unprecedented advancement has surpassed everyone's expectations, and it's clear to all that they require no further assistance. They're free and independent states who are recognized as such by their father nation, the United States, who has twice won independence for the freedom and liberty of all people, Earthen or otherwise. Their great success has inspired hope in the hearts of Americans, and has once again rekindled a spirit of adventure and manifest destiny across the United States. We've only begun to explore humanity's final frontier, and with God at the helm we will spread life to the four corners of the universe. God's incredible gift of life will exist in every star system, in every galaxy, in every galactic cluster for all time. Mankind was created to inherit the stars, and to obtain stewardship over creation. I am growing old and my life is nearing it's end. I've done this work with Christ my Savior in mind, and I hope to rejoice with Him soon. Once I'm gone, I pray my successors will continue my work in earnest, with thankfulness unto God. It is by His divine authority that we are even allowed to take our next breath, and He has seen it fit that His children should populate other worlds. We owe an incredible debt to all those who came before us. Our ancestors conquered lands, spread the good news of the gospel far and wide, developed incredible technologies by the grace of the Almighty and gave their lives in defense of all that we cherish. Without their selfless devotion and sacrifices, we could not have

dreamed of arriving at this apex
of civilization. As we grow ever
closer to discovering the hidden
secrets of God's creation, a fire
has been ignited in each of us, a
childlike wonder of what
incredible things lie just beyond
the veil of the night sky. Just as
Abraham looked up in amazement at
the number of visible stars above
when pondering God's covenant,
that same sense of awe and wonder
has been awakened in all of
mankind. Many millions of men and
women back on Earth desire the
opportunity to become colonists
and explore and tame inconceivably
distant worlds. The era of
history's middle children has long
since ended, and a new era of
exploration, voyaging,
cartography, and pioneering has
begun. This is a day our fathers,
grandfathers, and even 3rd great
grandfathers couldn't have
imagined. Historically, eras of

Christian enlightenment are always followed by periods of unprecedented societal and technological growth, though the following collapse and moral decay that typically follows is much more profound and incredibly destructive. There is no doubt among anyone that the prophecy that Christ revealed to John in Revelation will occur as it is written, meaning human morality will eventually decay once more, but these past few decades seem to have been a slight break in the birthing pains, an ongoing calm before the most drastic downpour of wrath and calamity ever witnessed by any being. For now, mankind is properly obeying the Word of God, and as He as promised, He has blessed the many nations of the world.

EPILOGUE

As stated previously, this is the complete account of the famed MOSS Colony "Hat Man" incident, as it has been posthumously dubbed, along with many other incredible historical events just as my ancestor, Dr. John Duncan, recorded them in his official logbook. Each page has been carefully scanned in full detail to retain it's original typewriter-like font for your enjoyment, while also preserving the original document. As the USDIH director, I've had the privilege of delving into many other classified historical documents over the previous few months, one of which is a handwritten account of the Second American Revolutionary War written by Edward G. Duncan. While the original manuscript itself is too faded to be properly photocopied and formatted for publishing, there exists many typed copies which have been perfectly transcribed from the original. I plan to *finally* declassify this incredible work for the educational benefit of all Americans. Our nation's history should be cherished by all and preserved for time immemorial. As you

read this work, give thanks and remember the
incredible gifts God has given mankind. -Silas
Duncan, USDIH Director, 05-28-2278

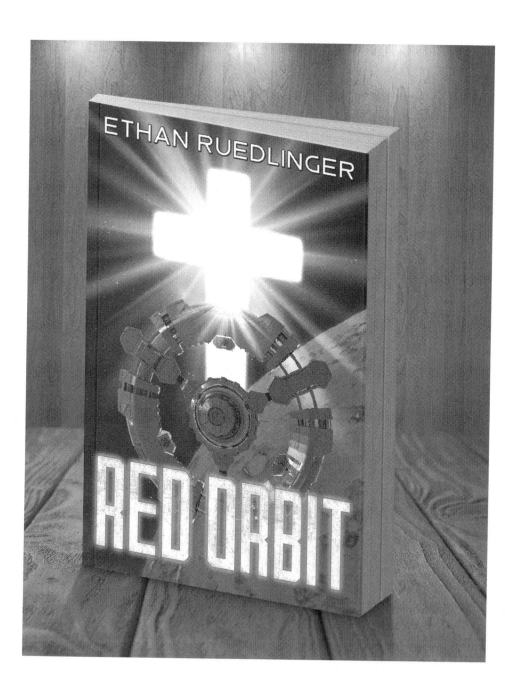

A Record Of The Notable Ancestry
Of The Ruedlingers

The *known* Ruedlinger family history spans dozens of generations, across hundreds of families, with hundreds of stories recorded for the future generations of Ruedlingers (& other eventual descendants of mine who don't share my last name) who would like to know where they came from, who their ancestors are, and/or are proud of their ancestry. I happen to be one of them, and as the current sole heir of my father's Ruedlinger family name, I have decided to take it upon myself to record and catalogue our family's history for my descendants, just as many generations before me have generously devoted their time to recording my ancestors' family's history for my knowledge and enjoyment.

Mom & Dad

My parents were born about 56 and 54 years before me. They were born and raised in a much different world, an entirely separate cultural and technological time period. Their 1950's childhood differs immensely from my early 2000's childhood. I would go as far as to say that the generational gap between my parents' generation and mine is the largest in recorded history, as the vast majority of generations throughout recorded history never experienced any substantial technological growth or scientific advancement, especially nowhere near the levels the modern generations of the 20th and 21st centuries have. Because of this major and historically unprecedented leap in technology, their history, their way of life, their knowledge, and experiences are set to evaporate within the next few decades. This is why it is important to record their history now.

In this book, I'll discuss the issues threatening our nation and our freedom in greater detail and explain why it is important for our generation to restore traditional American values!

God's Plan: 100 Days Of Bible Study

This book is a daily reading plan meant to strengthen your understanding of the Bible and give you insights into the deeper meaning of God's Word. For 100 days, you'll learn the Word of God with a daily Bible verse and explanation of it's meaning. Enrich your knowledge of the Bible with this easy-to-read daily Bible Verse book!

The Story Of Ethan Ruedlinger
Volume 1: Shambles

This is the story of Ethan Ruedlinger, A man who lived many different lives. A man who's life collapsed into shambles in a matter of days. The life he built for himself, gone for good, leaving him to cope with it's loss. He attempts to use his new situation as an opportunity to rise from the ashes, to launch himself from rock bottom. However, he quickly discovers it's not as easy as he'd hoped to simply "start over."

The Story Of Ethan Ruedlinger
Volume 2: Forever You'll Be

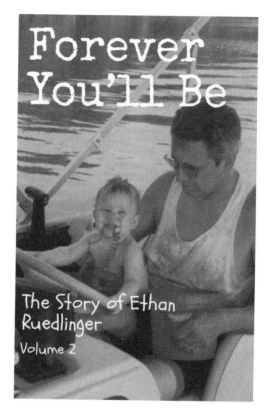

This is the second installment in the "The Story of Ethan Ruedlinger" autobiographical series, and traces back my adopted lineage, my biological lineage, and my early life; my infancy, my childhood, and my teen years. Each installment in this series is a memoir of sorts. A snapshot of people, places, and events now lost in the sands of time, living on only in the hearts and memories of those who still remain to tell their stories.

The Story Of Ethan Ruedlinger
Volume 3: No Man's Road

When the cruel hand of betrayal inevitably comes knocking, we must leave the ones who've wronged us behind and continue on toward a better future. We have no choice but to leave the past in the past and keep moving forward, no matter how difficult the road may be. Sometimes, if we're lucky, we may bump into someone along the way who will walk the rest of the road with us. This is my journey down "No Man's Road."

The Story Of Ethan Ruedlinger
Volume 4: The Walmart Chronicles

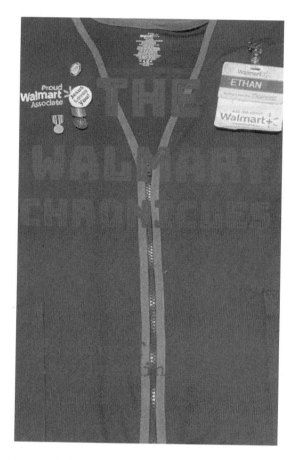

This book is a journal. A continuation of my autobiographical series chronicling the ins and outs of my daily life while working in the hostile work environment of a certain ultra-greedy American corporation.

The Story Of Ethan Ruedlinger
Volumes 1-4

Each installment in this series is a memoir of sorts. A snapshot of people, places, and events now lost in the sands of time, living on only in the hearts and memories of those who still remain to tell their stories. This series accurately portrays the life of Ethan Wayne Ruedlinger. Everything in this book is entirely factual to the best of my knowledge, and has been checked against several sources.

For More Reading Materials, Visit: www.amazon.com & Search: Ethan Ruedlinger!

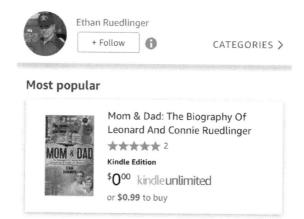
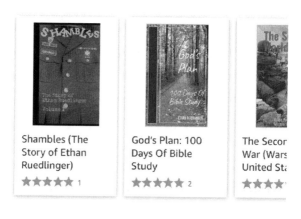

WHAT'S NEXT FOR AUTHOR ETHAN RUEDLINGER?

As teased by the epilogue of this book, the next book I'll be publishing will effectively be a prequel to this work. Within, we will ponder a scenario in which the United States in it's current form has grown so politically, economically, and societally tumultuous that the only recourse for American citizens is to take up arms against the jaws of the tyrannical regime which is attempting to devour them. Before freedoms can be restored, and tranquillity savored, there must be bloodshed as a consequence of the greed and selfish ambition of tyrants. In the following pages, I'll share an excerpt from the preliminary manuscript for:

The Second Civil War

The men of our great nation weren't always in a state of such patriotism and selfless devotion to freedom. I can recall a day when Americans possessed no inherent loyalty to the constitution, no admiration of American culture or values, no respect for their fellow countrymen. I remember a time prior to the war when we were, at first, treated as indentured servants by the "regime", as it's now commonly referred to by most, gradually worsening until we were no more significant than cattle, ready to be led to slaughter. It is my hope that by a miracle of God it would one day seem the "2ACW" is but a distant memory in the hearts and minds of the younger generations of Americans. Those of us that survive this war will still bear the scars, and thankfully the benefits, of a hard-fought victory. I plan to give a complete account here of my time serving in The Constitutional Army to the present time.

I'll begin in 2027, after a brief agreement between the US Government and an organization dedicated to preserving the American way of life that was so blatantly disregarded by both parties, it barely warrants a mention, yet this agreement played a crucial role as the ultimate catalyst for this war. Both sides had substantial political authority, both sides were initially threatening each other with legal and civil action. To sidestep a potential armed conflict, they had both compromised on issues such as border security, immigration, abortion, and gay rights; and both sides had violated these agreements by continuing to push their agendas on the masses through lobbying and threatening civil war should their demands not be met.

America's federal government had been tightening the shackles around the working class for nearly a century through inflation, taxation, and the out of control federal reserve. Like a frog gradually boiling in water, many Americans were too blind to catch on to the reality of their situation, and their impending doom. The grandfathers of men born in the early 21st century lived comfortably in three bedroom houses on the salary of a convenience store clerk, never worrying about their next meal or how they would pay their bills on time, while the men of my generation often labored tirelessly simply to survive until their next paycheck. Many men worked themselves six feet into the ground, scratching and clawing at the edge of their cage of financial enslavement for an escape that didn't exist. Naturally, usury gradually became a more frequent practice in all transactions, perhaps not as a side effect of the nation's subversion, but one of many weapons yielded by our authoritarian regime which had been installed to bring us to our knees. As the economy worsened and inflation reached an unfathomable height of 48% annually, essential commodities such as gasoline and water were financed, often with astronomically high interest rates far above 100%. We knew this way of life was unsustainable even for the upper middle class. We were tax cattle, meant to do nothing more than feed the very system that had enslaved us, and line the pockets of our task masters. We were subjugated by lesser men, being fed mind-altering chemicals through our food and water that would render us mindless "zombies." We were meant to be kept as passive, docile creatures who unwittingly labored solely for the benefit of the US Government and its wealthier benefactors and political figures, as well as the many large corporations which had inadvertently become the nation's second sovereign governing body, in retrospect it was likely due to the failure of a bill meant to abolish lobbying. As poverty ravaged the nation throughout the first quarter of the new millennium, many morally depraved men of ill intent gained power over the lower class, designing men who instituted intentionally disastrous policies to inflict psychological and financial suffering upon the American populace. The lines dividing the upper and lower class were further parted each year as the American middle class evaporated, fading into a distant memory of a bygone era. We were trapped in a two party political system, both controlled by the same deranged men, with the same intentionally detrimental ideological agenda, and the same ultimate goal in mind for the fate of America. Wether Republican, Independent, or Democrat;

Conservative, Libertarian, or Liberal, each politician rose to power only on the strings of the puppet-masters they served. The older generations were blind to the nefarious intentions of our silver tongued tyrants. The government-controlled American Media Complex would churn out soulless propaganda for the sole purpose of retaining control of the general public's conscious thought and political stance, manipulating public perception as if it were some sort of sick game. The media would consistently release articles and columns condemning certain individuals or groups of people, enacting a controlled "divide and conquer" scheme. The older generations often mocked and scorned the younger generation, labeling the "kids today" as nothing more than "lazy and ignorant", echoing each sentiment that the mainstream media embedded into their minds, much like many of the younger generation in a sense, who had been institutionally conditioned through government-dictated curriculums to believe the society they were born into was overflowing with hatred, violence, and inequality from its very foundation, judging the greatest men of history through a modern lens of morality. Many state and local governments, as well as large corporations had long ago cleansed the nation of any authentic artifacts or tangible tributes to its history. Anything, from statues of "dangerous individuals", to war relics "from a sensitive period in time", to paintings "depicting evil white men", to "insensitive" grocery store syrup bottles, butter sticks and rice boxes, they had either been altered or destroyed entirely as to reduce the likelihood of cultivating any healthy attitudes toward America's history among the youth. Without any solid evidence that the government hadn't already erased, they swallowed each lie that was fed to them. Even so, they were ruthlessly mocked. Yes, the men who'd seen a better time, the men belonging to a bygone era of relative peace and prosperity raised their voices in the public square as they denounced the youth of their nation in ignorance, who were now begging and pleading for mercy, to be spared enslavement at the hands of a merciless ruling class who'd forced each of them into extreme poverty for the sake of exploiting their perpetual labor while minimizing their consumption of the resources they produced. In a historically unprecedented turn of events, the baby boomer generation had built their own lives of prosperity without any concern for their future descendants, and pulled the ladder up behind them, burning the ladder to retain their comfort and wealth until the day of their departure from this world.

-The Second Civil War, Chapter 1: The Compromise Of 1850... In 2027

Made in the USA
Columbia, SC
26 October 2024

44892547R00146